Mission in Paris
1990

SEQUEL TO *HEARTS ON FIRE, PARIS 1968*

Bill Pearl

Fifty Years Late Publishing

Fifty Years Late Publishing
https://www.billpearl.net
USA Copyright Registered

Paperback ISBN: 978-0-9972927-2-5
E-book ISBN: 978-0-9972927-3-2

Cover Photo: Composite Place des Vosges, Paris, France and The Citadel, Hue, Vietnam
Back Cover Photo: Ngoc Son Temple on Jade Island Hanoi, Vietnam
© 2020 Bill Pearl

First printing 2021

To my mother, Helen

Prologue

"You could buy a Rolls-Royce for what I paid for this bottle." Robert Samberg shrugged and smiled as he held up the bottle with a hand-drawn label, *Macallan 1926,* at the bar at the Hotel Crillon.

A shapely Vietnamese woman in a sheer black silk dress that left little to the imagination moved to the leather barstool next to his. "Just how much?" she asked coyly as she took the bottle and placed her hand lightly on Robert's knee.

"A Silver Cloud...vintage... that's how much."

"What year?" she asked.

"You know about Silver Clouds?" Her soft, sultry voice had garnered Samberg's full attention.

She smiled. "I've been in a few."

He smiled.

"Or...the down payment on a stallion—mine just won the Kentucky Derby—made a fortune," Robert said and took back the bottle.

"You love that horse?" she asked as she slid her hand from his knee up along his thigh.

"I do. Beauty, high value, good listener, a loyal friend—rare as this bottle of *Macallan.* That's what I call him."

The barman approached—Robert's old friend, Pierre Le Rest, a large, jovial, mustachioed Frenchman from Nice. He was a veteran of the French War in Indochina, who used to wait on Robert during his student days in the Latin Quarter in 1968. Twenty-two years had passed, and Pierre had moved to the high temple of old-world Paris elegance, the bar at the Hotel Crillon, where he catered to Robert's every need like a doting uncle and manservant.

"Robert is celebrating, mademoiselle," Pierre said. "He just bought fifty radio stations in America. You're sitting next to the owner of America's largest broadcast company."

He poured another round for Robert and one for his new female acquaintance.

Robert held up his glass. "This is the *Glencairn* glass, designed with one purpose."

"Which is...?" she asked.

"To capture the aroma. Look at the shape, the taper," he gushed. Then, raising his glass, he bellowed, "To the Samberg Group!"

She, too, held up her glass and clinked his. They imbibed the rare single malt whisky and followed it with a swig of spring water.

"Only twelve bottles in the world!" Pierre said.

"So smooth!" she smiled and snuggled closer.

Pierre brought over a plate of hors d'oeuvres and looked at Robert. "Could you have imagined this in 1968?"

"Of course, I knew all along," he said as he winked and lifted his arms like a maestro leading an orchestra.

"Oh yes, I remember that scruffy student leader throwing cobble-stone," Pierre said as he turned to address the smiling mademoiselle. "Robert was quite the radical in those days. He led the charge on Rue Saint-Jacques. A real hero!"

"I don't know that street. I'm from Hanoi," she whispered.

"Hanoi?" Robert looked up at her. "I have a friend—uh, *had* a friend in Hanoi."

"What's the name?"

"We lost touch." His voice dropped, signaling his unwillingness to provide any additional information.

"He opposed the war, too—way before most Americans," Pierre said in an obvious attempt to raise his friend's suddenly sagging spirits.

"I knew the war was a disaster. I knew it," Robert said.

"The American War? That's what we Vietnamese called it."

"We called it the Vietnam War—a tragedy by any name," he said.

"I was just a child," she replied as she sighed and ran her tiny fingers through her long black hair.

Robert laughed, then turned to her. "I was a student back then, and I tried to stop it." He looked off in the distance, past the confines of the gilded bar room to images of a jungle exploding from napalm. It was a dreadful scene from a dream he'd had again and again.

Recognizing the stress on his face, she gently poked him.

"Hey, come on back," she said playfully. "What did you do? Throw cobblestones, set cars on fire?"

"I met in that room with a member of Vietnam's Politburo." Robert pointed. "Right over there."

"That sounds—well, I wasn't...how do you say, born yesterday?"

"No, it's true—we had dinner right over there." He pointed to the table by the window.

"Was My Hanh there?" Pierre asked.

Robert shifted awkwardly on his barstool.

"Your friend?" she asked.

Robert looked away. "Let's break open another bottle!"

Pierre chimed in. "Robert, we only have four left—maybe take your time?"

A bellman approached. "Monsieur, you have a long-distance call from Washington. You can take it at the front desk."

Robert got up and followed the bellman to the lobby. He was steady on his feet despite having drunk so much—a skill he'd developed over the years.

The bellman handed him the phone.

"What's up?" he yelled into the receiver.

"What's up with *you*, sweetheart?" It was Allen Hoffers, Robert's old boss in the Senate, now the Undersecretary of State for South Asia and a top advisor to Secretary of State James Baker.

"Sweetheart, eh?"

"Yeah—you made that sweetheart deal."

"How the hell did you find me?"

"Andi—that efficient wife of yours!" She was also the executive vice president of Robert's company and handled the details of both their personal and professional lives. "I ran into her at Clyde's in Georgetown, having lunch with one of your attorneys...Jack, somebody..."

Robert laughed. He pulled the phone away from his ear. *Damn, I asked her to keep the trip private! The bitch never gets it right!*

"Have you been drinking?" Allen asked.

"Celebrating!"

"The case of *Macallan 1926*... I heard about that. Cost you almost as much as the stations!"

"How do you know?"

"*Wine Spectator*—a big spread," Allen said.

"The press loves me! Speak up, the connection sucks!"

Allen raised his voice. "I hear you fine."

"Remember when I called you from the post office in the Latin Quarter?"

In 1968 when he was in trouble. In those days, you had to go to the post office to make a transatlantic call.

"No espionage on this visit, I hope," Allen said.

And back then, as he was certain Allen remembered, he had passed secret intelligence to Allen that could have changed the outcome of the presidential election that year.

"Why are you calling...Mr. Undersecretary?"

"Well, I wanted to congratulate you on the radio deal of the century!"

"The millennium . . ."

"Okay, the millennium!"

"You're talking to America's radio tycoon!"

"How's your father?" Allen asked.

"Unhappy I bought his radio station."

"He'll get over it."

"You don't know my father. What's happening at State?" Robert asked.

"Got our hands full with Saddam Hussein."

"Eyeing the black gold in Kuwait?"

"Afraid so. We're doing contingencies if he crosses the line."

"What, you guys didn't get enough war in Vietnam? Now you want to fight Arabs!"

"All in a day's work for a superpower," Allen said.

"Did you see the Hubble photo?" Robert glanced at the cover of a French weekly magazine on the front desk that showed the first photo of our galaxy from the space telescope.

"All that tax money and we got a blurry photo."

"NASA should have put you in charge."

"Well, if they had, it wouldn't be blurry," Robert said.

"I have no doubt."

"Hey, anything else? I've got a celebration going on here."

"There are a couple of things we need to discuss," Allen said.

"Like what?"

"Not on the phone."

"Ooh, top secret shit?"

"Can you stop in D.C. on your way home?"

"I can do that."

"Good, I'll get your return flight from Andi and arrange a meeting."

"Okay, Boss—now can I go back to my party?"

"Good night, Robert!"

"Bye, Allen!"

Robert handed the phone back to the bellman, then lingered for a moment and gazed at the ancien régime decor of the lobby—the glass chandeliers, ornately painted ceiling, and reliefs bordering the marble walls.

What couple of things? He tapped his index finger on the front desk. Then, he returned to the bar and handed Pierre a wad of Francs, nodding to the empty stool where his new friend had been.

"Is it arranged?" Robert asked, with the look of a teenage boy in heat.

"Yes, another twenty minutes—"

"Is that enough?" He looked at the money.

"More than enough," Pierre smiled as he fetched the bottle of

Macallan and poured another round. Robert savored the aroma, then drank the glass as if it were a cheap shot. He felt the hot flush of the whisky. He glanced at his watch repeatedly, rose from his stool, and before departing, looked over to the window table where he, My Hanh, and her father, Thành, had sat on that evening in May long ago. Her smile flashed before his eyes; her voice still whispered to him. He shook his head, trying to block out the memories, and made his way upstairs to the suite.

He unlocked the door and walked in.

The stunning mademoiselle lay naked across the king-size bed. He dove into her arms, devouring her without once looking at her face.

Chapter 2

Robert sat on a blue silk Chippendale chair in the majestic, colonial-style waiting room outside the office of the secretary of state. He flipped through the April issue of *Town & Country* magazine he'd taken from the coffee table in front of him. He wore a navy blazer, tan cashmere slacks, an alligator belt and shoes, legs crossed, and his right loafer hanging from his bronzed bare foot. He flexed the foot back and forth, nonstop, and wiped the sweat from his palms on the arms of the chair.

Allen Hoffers entered the room dressed in a dark blue business suit, red tie, and brown wingtips—standard State Department attire. Robert rose to greet him.

"My, we're Florida casual," Allen said. "No socks?" He raised an eyebrow. Allen was never bashful about parenting his old friend.

"Hey, old pal!" Robert gripped his hand tightly and moved their joined hands up and down in a rapid motion. "Socks are *out* in Palm Beach."

"Rough flight? You look tired, man."

"No rest for the weary!"

"All those stations…that was some accomplishment," Allen said, proud of Robert.

"Like winning the Derby all over again!" Robert raised his voice and lifted himself on his toes.

Allen was also at the top of his game. He had capitalized on his relationship with the now-retired Senator Lance Hanke, once the powerful Chairman of the Foreign Relations Committee and protégé of President Lyndon Johnson. He moved to the State Department, where he rose to the top of the ranks.

Secretary of State James Baker arrived, accompanied by Senators John McCain and John Kerry. Allen made the introductions, and they entered the secretary's mahogany-paneled private office.

"There's something I need to tell you," Allen whispered to Robert as they arrived at a cluster of colonial-style armchairs by the fireplace near the secretary's desk.

Damn, there he goes again, telling me there's something he needs to say to me. Annoying!

"So?" Robert asked. "What is it?"

Before Allen could respond, Secretary Baker started the meeting. "Congratulations on the Kentucky Derby."

"Thank you, Mr. Secretary."

"And I hear you're about to become America's number one radio company."

"Yes, Mr. Secretary, as soon as the FCC approves the transfers." Robert pointed at two portraits on the wall next to Baker's desk. "I see you have John Jay and Thomas Jefferson keeping an eye on us."

"Yes, we're in good company! I've had many visitors recognize Jefferson, but you're the first to identify Jay," Baker said.

"I've read the history."

"Ahh, and there's Robert Livingston." Robert pointed at another portrait behind Baker's desk. "I read Livingston's correspondence when I did my thesis at the Library of Congress."

Baker looked wide-eyed at Allen and the senators.

"I told you, he's the man for the job!" Allen said proudly.

"What job?" Robert asked, his interest piqued.

"Robert, I think we can help each other," Secretary Baker said in a low-key diplomatic manner.

"Go on," Robert said, intrigued but cautious.

"The president has received a feeler from someone he trusts about reconciling with Vietnam—it came from a member of the Politburo."

"Really?" *My God, could it be Thành?*

Baker pulled a red file from the top drawer of the desk and opened it. We know your history with Vietnam's legendary leader Le Duc

Thành and his daughter in May 1968."

"That's ancient history," Robert said dismissively. "I haven't seen them for twenty years."

"Twenty-two, to be exact. You helped Thành. You passed on his message about Nixon's interference in the peace talks before the '68 presidential election."

"The election won by Nixon," Robert said as if to profess innocence. *This guy probably voted for the crook.*

"Yes, well, some people will not be happy about restoring relations, which is why the president wants this handled quietly by a civilian. We're not ready to put our fingerprints on it. Do you understand?"

"Yes." *I don't like where this is going.* Robert began to tap the arm of his chair with his index finger.

"Of course, we don't know the feeler is from Thành. It could be from someone else. Thành retired. He has cancer."

"What about My Hanh?" Robert said as he looked at Allen, who knew their history.

"She's a rising star in the party, advisor to the chairman."

"I'm not surprised. She was ambitious and capable back in '68." *And broke my heart.*

"The move makes sense after the border war with China. They're looking for protection," Senator Kerry said, his voice certain, his tall, thin frame barely fitting in his chair. Until now, Kerry and McCain had both sat silently.

"A reconciliation will serve our interests and theirs. It will help us get back the remains of our soldiers," McCain said. He was the American hero who'd refused an offer of early release from prison in Hanoi due to his father's rank as admiral, and chose instead to wait his turn like any other soldier. *A son inspired by his father...not in my family!*

"They also want the trade embargo ended, and if we do that, it will open their market for our manufacturers," Allen added.

"We have as much to fear from China as Vietnam does," Robert said.

"Very observant, Mr. Samberg," Baker said.

"I read *Foreign Affairs Magazine.*"

"Right—well, the president wants to open a backchannel to explore ending the trade embargo and opening relations. Will you take this on?"

"Mr. Secretary, I'm a businessman."

"Allen tells me you taught yourself Vietnamese, you know the history, you're a civilian, unknown in foreign policy circles—at least in this century." They all laughed.

"You know I'm a Democrat?" Baker nodded and smiled at Senator Kerry. "No matter."

"Ho Chi Minh once asked us to support Vietnam's independence," Robert pointed out. "He was moved by Roosevelt's stirring words about ending colonial rule after the Second World War. We let them down. Then we fought a bloody war. Why should they trust us?" Robert asked.

"Robert, history is filled with stories of nations that fought bitter wars and made peace afterward, when their interests required it," Baker said.

"I guess this *could* be another of those moments," Robert said, his tone skeptical.

Baker leaned over his desk. "The mission is to find out if this *is* one of those moments."

I put all this behind me...My Hanh, Vietnam, the war...taking this on will open up a can of worms...I'll get nothing out of it...unless...

"Hey, I'm flattered, I really am." Robert shook his head slowly. *I've got back-to-back meetings next week...the station managers, the finance people, the lawyers...*

"I'm very tied up right now."

"We're not talking about a lot of time," Baker said. "You would travel to Hanoi under the cover of an exchange program, meet secretly with their representative, and learn what they want as part of a deal. It won't take long, maybe three to four days. Then report back to us."

"Do you guys have any idea what it takes to do a nationwide, multi-market acquisition?"

"For god's sake," Allen said, "this is for your country." He scolded Robert with his look, paused, then smiled. "Besides, who else could we get who knows how to buy fifty radio stations for the price of ten?"

Robert smiled broadly. *They love me.* "Right! I did put an amazing deal together."

"Robert, we need someone successful in the private sector," Baker said.

"Dare I ask what's in it for me?" Robert looked at Baker, Allen and the two senators who responded with looks of disappointment. "Hey, I'm a business guy!"

"Think of our military families," McCain said, lowering his voice as if offering a Sunday sermon. "We owe it to them to bring home the remains of our soldiers. This mission can start that process."

"What about the rights to construct broadcast towers in Vietnam once relations are established? Is that too much to ask?" Robert said.

"I think you're getting a little ahead of yourself, Robert." Secretary Baker looked at Allen as if ordering him to handle this.

"What about broadcast rights for American content? Surely they'll want American content down the road."

"Robert!" Allen barked, as if scolding an errant child.

Awkward silence.

"Robert, your station deal needs FCC approval, right?" Baker asked.

"Mr. Secretary, are you screwing with me?" Robert gripped the arms of his chair and looked at Allen. "Is there going to be a problem?"

"There could be," Allen responded.

"*Could* be?" Robert looked squarely at his old friend.

"Not from us." Allen raised his hand as if to hold him back.

"Then, from whom?"

"That's what I wanted to tell you." Allen's tortoise-shell glasses slipped down his nose.

"I prefer getting bad news quickly."

"You didn't hear this from us..." Allen leaned toward his friend.

"Hear what?" Robert shifted to the edge of his chair.

"Dick Dellmore has filed objections to your applications."

Allen's words struck him like a rattlesnake bite.

Dellmore was the head of Samcom, Robert's father's old company, whom his father had chosen over Robert years before to run the company after he retired.

"You left Samcom because of him, right?" Allen said.

"That son of a bitch!" Robert turned to Baker. "Mr. Secretary, I need those challenges to go away!"

"Well, you know, Robert, that's not our department . . ."

Allen looked at Baker and Robert, then broke the silence. "We'll have to see what kind of dirt they bring up—we could look into it."

Baker got up, reached out to shake Robert's hand, and repeated, "Yes, we could look into it."

"So, you'll go?" Allen asked.

Robert looked around the room. *No damn choice.* "Okay, I'll go make nice with Vietnam."

"Good!" Allen and Baker responded in unison. They walked toward the office door. Allen threw Robert a reassuring look.

"One condition. Next time, make peace with a country where they drink *Macallan* and have horse racing, okay?" Robert half-smiled.

On the way out, they passed portraits of John Adams and John Quincy Adams, side by side. Robert looked up at them. *Father and son presidents...ha, not in my fucking family!*

Chapter 3

"I'm Bao Dinh," said a tall man dressed in a blue *áo dài* robe and matching turban who was standing at the bottom of the ramp that led from the aircraft to the terminal of Hanoi's Noi Bai International Airport. He lowered a cardboard sign with Robert's name scrawled in red crayon and reached out for his hand.

Robert walked up to him. "Ah, Mr. Dinh, a fellow radio man! Nice to meet you." His cover for the mission was a State Department executive exchange program with Vietnam's national radio station, Voice of Vietnam.

Dinh did not know the true reason for his visit. He smiled. "I'm the Director of the Ministry of Information and Communications—welcome to Vietnam! I trust you had a good flight." His ministry ran the Voice of Vietnam.

Robert rolled his eyes. "It was a twenty-two-hour flight and I can't sleep on a plane."

"Not so good then, I imagine."

"You imagine right."

Dinh smiled again and turned his head. "Follow me, please." Flashing a metal ID card to the security guards, he led Robert past the cordoned lanes where other passengers lined up to pass through customs and immigration. They walked straight to the baggage area where a porter had Robert's luggage. The three of them exited the airport and walked to a black Volga limo.

Once in the back seat, Dinh turned to Robert. "I have been instructed to take you to meet Le Thi Suong, the woman in charge of your visit."

"It can't wait until tomorrow?"

13

"No, she wants to see you now."

Robert winced. "Do you have any idea how tired I am?"

"I do," Dinh replied, handing the driver a card with the address.

Robert sighed and stared out the car window. He spotted a young woman carrying a child in a pouch on her back. She wore a silk *áo* dài like the one My Hanh had worn two decades earlier on the Paris métro. He remembered their passion, the pregnancy, the child they were supposed to have. *She had an abortion! Robbed me of becoming a father. Damn! Chances are I won't even see her. I don't want to see her.*

It was October, the end of fall in Vietnam. It had rained all morning and the limo did not have air-conditioning. The humidity was insufferable, and Robert sweated right through his light-weight grey suit. They passed the Imperial Citadel of Thang Long and the Old City Gates. The red bricks at the base of the gates reminded him of the wall surrounding the Nanterre University courtyard where he and Danny the Red had charged CRS police lines in '68. *Foolish youth saving the world....* Robert gazed at the crowded streets filled with bicycles carrying things you never saw on bikes in America—chickens in crates, sacks of grain, a pig stretched out on a stake. He saw street vendors squatting on corners with their baskets of fruits and vegetables. He noticed the tangle of electric wiring outside every building they passed.

"They still don't have building codes here?"

"After the Christmas bombing in '72, we didn't have the luxury to think about building codes"

"I remember."

"It was the war," Dinh said with resignation.

"I know, I'm—I'm sorry..." Robert's decades-old outrage began to stir. He had really cared about this once. "So, how are things at the Voice of Vietnam?"

"We're looking forward to your visit, to learning how you operate America's largest radio company."

"You know about the acquisition?"

"Yes, we follow industry news around the world; you made quite the impression."

I've got so much work to do at home. I need to get in and get out of here fast!

The limo arrived at Hanoi's Old Quarter after following a maze of streets lined with French colonial architecture, Buddhist and Daoist temples with throngs of people moving about in organized chaos. It stopped in front of a modest row house. Robert and Dinh left the car and walked to the front door, greeted by an elderly housekeeper with a somber look. She led them to the living room, where Le Thi Suong rose to greet them warmly, but with a sad look on her face.

"Welcome," she said, holding out her hand. She was a middle-aged woman, with black hair pulled straight back and wearing a black dress and large round glasses.

"Mr. Samberg, I am sorry to delay your arrival at the hotel. I know you must be tired. Would you like some tea?"

"Yes, thank you." Suong nodded to the housekeeper, who fetched the tea and returned with a pitcher and a silver tray with cups and a plate of rice cookies. Robert spotted a row of framed photos on the mantel and stopped before one, the tableau of a man and his daughter in Paris in 1968. *It's Thành and My Hanh outside the Hotel Crillon! I took this with my Kodak Brownie.* He immediately realized this was the home of Le Duc Thành.

"I remember the day I took this photo," Robert told Suong. "It was only a few days after I rescued My Hanh in the métro."

"I know," Suong responded, "I was Comrade General Thành's secretary for many years. I know all about you. Please sit down, Mr. Samberg, I have some bad news. A few days ago, my dear Thành, our great revolutionary hero, died after a long battle with cancer. He knew you were coming today, and on his last night, as we spoke of his funeral arrangements, he asked me to request that you join the procession and speak at his memorial ceremony."

"Oh no! I am sorry to hear this. I knew he was ill, but I didn't realize…"

"It is a great loss for us."

"I admired him, and I'm disappointed I didn't come sooner."

"He admired you as well. He never forgot how you helped him in

1968. He thought you were brave," she said.

"Did you say speak at his ceremony?"

"Yes, it's a service at the funeral hall where people will come to pay their respects and top party leaders will celebrate his life. After, we'll join the procession to Mai Dich Cemetery, a special resting place for our revolutionary heroes." Robert felt the grim effects of too little sleep and too many whiskeys on the flight.

My god! "You mean today? You want me to speak like—now?"

I came here to save my radio deal, not to get pulled into the past. How can I turn off these thoughts about My Hanh if I must see her again...at her father's funeral no less?

"Yes. Exactly. The procession begins shortly, so if you agree, we'll need to leave."

He stood up and walked over to the photo of Thành and My Hanh. He lifted it from the shelf and examined it again. He thought of his conversations with Thành years before about the war and the day he told Thành he loved his daughter. *He was a good father. Loyal. He protected her. He supported her even though he opposed the relationship. He treated me with respect even though I was an American. He was firm in his beliefs, honest in expressing his thoughts but always gentle, with never a hint of unkindness. He was the father I always wanted and never had. He was the father I would never get to become.* "It would be an honor," Robert whispered.

"Mr. Samberg," Suong continued, "in Vietnam, we believe that every man must have a proper funeral so he can enter the afterlife. If he does not, his ghost will stay on Earth and can cause harm to his family. You have been honored by Thành's last wish; he would be happy to know you respected it."

Suong rose, walked over to Robert as he replaced the picture, and led him back outside, followed by Binh. The driver got out of the car, surprised to see them again so soon. Binh instructed him to take them to the funeral hall.

Robert sat in the back seat looking out at the tumult of the city. *Why this honor after so many years? What will I say?* Twenty minutes later, the car arrived at the gate to the funeral hall. The driver slowed as they moved alongside the crowds of people arriving to celebrate Thành's life before his burial.

"He touched many lives," Suong said. There was a large crowd in traditional black costumes, a sea of conical hats secured with silk chin straps—people arriving from all directions on bicycles ladened with fresh flowers, sacks of fruit, and bundles of incense to lay at Thành's altar.

The driver pulled over and they exited the car. Robert moved confidently through the crowd despite his fatigue, following Suong and Binh to the entrance of the hall where the ceremony was about to begin. He could hear the sound of drums and gongs from inside the building. An usher led the three of them to the second row just behind the leaders of the Communist Party and government. Robert expected to be treated coldly—a wealthy entrepreneur from the nation whose warplanes had dropped bombs on this nation just two decades before. Instead, to his surprise, he was greeted warmly. The country's top party cadres led tributes to Thành, with large red, yellow, and white floral wreaths, including Prime Minister Do Cẩn and Communist Party Chief Vo Chi Cung, who lit incense and bowed their heads before the altar.

Soon it was Robert's turn to go on stage. Suong rose to introduce him. "Before he died, our venerable hero, Comrade Le Duc Thành, asked that we hear today from an American, Mr. Robert Samberg," she said solemnly. The crowd murmured its surprise.

That was the shortest introduction ever!

Robert rose, his too-tired mind racing, and climbed the stairs leading to the altar, which was surrounded by rows of white flowers, pots of fruit, and urns of burning incense. He approached Thành's casket draped with a red silk cloth and adorned with a single yellow star. He imagined the face of the man he once knew—rice and coins in his mouth now, the tradition. These and other offerings were for the life after death.

He planted a stick of incense in the urn in front of the altar, walked slowly around the coffin, and turned toward the podium across from him. *What to say?* Before him lay a sea of silent faces. He remembered the day long ago when he spoke for Danny the Red on rue Saint-Jacques in Paris—no script, only the passion of the moment to gather his thoughts and find the right words. *I knew this man...what he was made of...what a loss he must be. I must find the passion again.* Robert thought of Thành and his kindness, the trust that grew between them. It all came back to him, rolling across his consciousness like a wave. *Speak from your heart!* The music stopped as he reached the podium and placed his hands on either side to steady himself.

"Thành devoted his entire life to the independence of your nation. His contributions are legendary. His passing is a huge loss to your state, your people and your party. Years ago, when Vietnam was at war with America, I had the honor of meeting him as he tried to bring peace to both our lands. I thought at the time that his heart might be filled with hate for America. It would have been understandable. But it was not so. He did not give way to hate even as he engaged with the enemy. He once told me that forgiveness after war was possible, even though it was difficult. 'Life brings change,' he told me. 'Seasons change. Governments change. People change.' I can hear his voice telling me these things. Speaking wisdom. So, as an American, I am honored—" Robert paused, unable to find the words in Vietnamese to express his next thought. The room fell silent. He glanced down at a row of chairs off to the side of the stage, a place of honor where family members sat, dressed in white, and he glimpsed the familiar figure of a woman rising up like a mirage in the mist, then suddenly coming into focus—her face luminescent, her expression sad, dignified, caring. My Hanh looked up at him, as if nothing had changed in two decades. Robert gasped. He could not halt the swell of emotion, his eyes catching hers exactly as they once had on the Paris *métro*, his voice now locked in his throat. He watched as she tilted her head to the left ever so slightly, speaking volumes with her eyes as she used to do. And there next to her, tall like her, stately like her, stood a strapping young man. *No, it cannot be. It's not possible. The face. It's not just Vietnamese. It's also...my god! The green eyes. They're mine. They're mine.*

Chapter 4

His remarks had gone well. At the close of the service, Robert stood in the crowd of dignitaries introducing himself to everyone around him. His energy was back. He worked the room like a visiting ambassador. At the same time, he felt a nervous excitement about greeting My Hanh and the young man he thought was their son. Years before, he had mourned the loss of this child, believing My Hanh when she said she was going to terminate the pregnancy. He'd obsessed about whether it would have been a boy or a girl. He'd imagined their faces. He wrestled with guilt about not having followed her to save the child and their love. He'd passed through stages of denial, anger, depression, and acceptance. Now he was face to face with a past he had long buried. The life he thought had been taken from him suddenly seemed possible again.

Accompanied by Suong, Robert joined the mourners at the receiving line of family and dignitaries. She introduced him to Vo Chi Cung, Chairman of Vietnam's Council of State. My Hanh stood next to Cung, and Suong introduced her as Madame Delaunay, and the man next to her—as her husband, Bertrand and his son, An.

Her husband! His Son! Why not their son? What is this?

Robert extended his hand. My Hanh's arm rose slowly, the sleeve of her white outfit stretching to reveal her petite, perfectly formed hand. *Her skin is without flaw, no different than when I last saw her. After two decades, not a blemish!* Their eyes met, their hands touched, and they shook once in silence before My Hanh pulled away. He noticed the strength of her grip, more like a man's. This surprised him.

"Thank you for honoring my father's wishes." She spoke in that demure, melodious voice he remembered so well.

19

"It was my honor." *Can she hear my heart beating out of my chest?*

Suong moved Robert forward in the line, and he extended his hand to Bertrand, whom Suong introduced as a French diplomat, the consular officer at the French embassy in Kuwait. He smiled warmly and spoke with a French accent. "The old friend of my wife from Paris."

"Yes," Robert said, "...from Paris." He searched Bertrand's face for any resemblance to An. His eyes were brown, not green. There was a moment of awkward silence before Suong moved Robert along to the next person in line, An.

Robert's pulse raced. His palms sweat. "Nice to meet you," he said, brushing his hand on his trousers before extending it to An. *He looks a bit different up close, more Asian than Caucasian. Is he my son or Bertrand's?*

An shook his hand, holding it loosely, an obligatory coupling, and said nothing. His look was cold, his body language stiff.

Why so cold? "I knew your grandfather in Paris. He was a remarkable man." *Surely, I can reach him through Thành! His memory can be our starting point.*

Robert looked into An's eyes, but he lowered his head and averted them. *Could I be wrong about this? Certainly, she would have told me if she had had our child.*

Suong again moved Robert forward. There were others to meet. The pleasantries of the receiving line continued, the encounters stilted, perfunctory, anti-climactic. *I need to learn the truth about An.*

The burial ceremony at Mai Dich Cemetery was followed by a reception at Thành's home where Suong had prepared an altar and had supervised the preparation of a meal for family and dignitaries, copious plates of chicken, ham, pork, rice and desserts. Robert worked the room, introducing himself and keeping an eye out for My Hanh, who moved from conversation to conversation with others but did not return to him. He looked for An.

Why isn't he here?

Asked why he was visiting Vietnam, Robert kept to his script—the executive exchange program. Following the meal, his fatigue caught up with him. He told Suong that he needed to go to the hotel. She thanked him warmly for coming, for speaking, and organized a ride. She handed him a carefully wrapped gift, a book that, she explained, Thành wanted him to have.

He arrived at the Metropole Hotel where his baggage had already been delivered and unpacked. It was nearly 11 o'clock. He settled in, fueled by fumes of adrenalin and the excitement of the day's events. He sat for a moment at the edge of the bed, the linens already turned down for the night and lowered his head. *Why didn't she spend more time with me? What did she think of me? Did she feel anything? She's married. We're both married. I don't know what to make of An. Why did Suong call him Bertrand's son instead of their son?*

After a shower, Robert opened the minibar and grabbed two small bottles of scotch, pouring them into a tall glass. *UGH! Dewar's White Label!* He laughed. As a poor student in Paris, he used to drink Dewar's, which back then was top of the line. *All things were possible back then...even liking crappy scotch.* He sank into an easy chair in the living room, sipped his drink and heard a noise coming from the other room. It was the sound of a hotel usher sliding a note under the door. He walked over to pick it up, passing the clothes and shoes he had thrown on the floor before showering. He tore open the envelop, finding a handwritten message inside.

> Dear Robert,
> Thanks for your words today. You lifted our spirits at a sad time. Let's meet tomorrow at the Statue of Lý Thái Tổ beside Hoan Kiem Lake at 5:00 am. We can walk along the lake. An is coming, too. Vietnam is still within you, its mysteries awaiting to reveal more.
> My Hanh

Well, that's more like it! And she's bringing An. Yes! He must *be ours!* Robert put down the scotch, climbed into his pajamas, and collapsed on the bed. He dreamed of a ride he once took as a boy with his father on the Cyclone, the iconic wooden roller coaster on Coney Island in Brooklyn, New York. The coaster veered hard to the left and the right, twisting and turning and pressing him against the side of the flimsy carriage. He closed his eyes and grabbed his father's arm for protection. Then, as it chugged to its highest point, the chains pulling it grinding against the gears, the people and buildings in the amusement park below dwindling in scope and size, he opened his eyes and watched in horror as his father stood up, grabbed him, and tried to throw him out of the carriage. He awakened as he groped for his father's sleeve, his right arm thrashing the pillow he customarily hugged while sleeping, his breathing labored, his pajamas soaked with sweat.

Ah, damn, my father again! He haunts me. He looked at the clock. 1:30 am. He took a half tab of Ambien and went back to sleep.

The alarm rang at 4:00. Robert opened his eyes, released the pillow, and shook off the lingering effects of the Ambien and the bad dream. *A twenty-two-hour plane ride, four hours sleep, and now off to see My Hanh and An! Oy!* He jumped out of bed, threw cold water on his face, nibbled on the complimentary fruit plate provided as a welcome gift the previous day, dressed in tan shorts, a white polo and sneakers, and called the front desk for a large black coffee to go and a cycle rickshaw to take him to the lake. The breeze felt good on his face and the bumps in the road jarred him. Bicycles were the primary mode of transportation in Hanoi, though rapidly being replaced by motorbikes. Robert gazed at the crowds of people doing yoga, stretching, dancing, and roller skating in front of the statue of Vietnam's emperor Lý Thái Tổ at an hour when he and most Americans would still be asleep in bed.

"Hello," My Hanh said, as she swirled around from the back of the statue on her skates, stopped abruptly, and looked squarely at him. She was dressed in a tight-fitting exercise outfit that showed her toned body and, in the skates, was an inch or so taller than Robert. She did not smile.

"Hi," he said and stepped closer her. "You look—"

"Sad, I know. I did not sleep well. I dreamed about my father, the loss."

"I'm sorry." *She too? Her dream couldn't have been as bad as mine.*

"He used to tell me that life after death depends on how you live your life now."

"He led a good life," Robert said.

"Yes, and I celebrate that goodness at his altar, but the loss is painful."

Robert wanted to embrace her but he held himself back.

"Do you want to rent skates or walk?" she asked.

"Let's walk," he said. "I'm still dealing with travel fatigue."

My Hanh sat on the curb of the plaza to remove her skates.

"Where's An?" he asked anxiously.

"We're meeting him at the restaurant."

Looking at her, he said, "You're in better shape today than twenty-two years ago."

She smiled. "I work out—a lot."

"I don't," he said as he touched his stomach.

My Hanh looked up at the statue of the emperor. "He was a reformer, like your Robert Kennedy would have been."

"I never got to work for Kennedy." Robert recalled that My Hanh had suggested he join the Kennedy campaign when he returned home from Paris in 1968.

"I know. He was shot. So sad—another great loss. Lý Thái Tổ is my political hero. He was an expert in military tactics and martial arts, led the army on the battlefield to quell rebellions, reformed the government bureaucracy, and established a national university. Too bad he wasn't female."

"Still the woman's libber, huh?" Robert chuckled.

"I'm going to be the first woman elected chairman of the party."

"I don't doubt it." He smiled, still attracted to her ambition.

"It's my mission." She looked at him as if to gauge the sincerity of his reaction.

"I've dropped out of the competition for statues, though I can afford to put one—a large one—anywhere I want."

"What happened to the modest American I used to know?"

"I've come to believe that if you want something, you go for it—you just do it."

"You have changed."

"Haven't you?" Robert asked.

"Yes, life does that to you." The two of them walked along the path that hugged the lake and came upon a martial arts class. They stopped to observe a young girl in position to break a one-inch-thick board with her right hand. She came down hard, but the board did not break. Disappointment fell over her face.

My Hanh walked up to the girl and offered a word of encouragement. Then she stacked two more boards on top of the first, spun around, and in a flash, her palm struck the boards, breaking them apart. "Remember," she whispered to the young girl, who had an amazed look on her face, "it's in the breathing and the believing."

"Wow!" Robert exclaimed.

"I told you, I work out, a lot," she said.

They continued to walk in silence, soaking up the early morning sunlight, the sights and sounds of people enjoying the lakefront.

Should I ask?

"About An. Is he—?"

"Is he what?" she said.

"I mean, when I looked at his face, I saw—"

"Your eyes...green eyes," she said.

"He *is* our son!" he said.

She stopped and locked her ankles. "Yes—I didn't—I couldn't have the abortion," My Hanh said, speaking slowly as if to weigh every word.

"Why didn't you tell me?"

"How could I do that? You were 8,000 miles away. Our nations were at war."

"You should have told me. You should have found a way."

"It was complicated. There was more involved than just the two of us."

"What is more important than a father knowing he has a son?"

"In my family, I could not be mother to a *bui doi*. Nor could my father, a hero of the nation, suffer that fate."

"*Bui doi?*"

"Dust of life—it's what we call Amerasian children."

"So, you gave birth to a son who was 'dust' to you?"

"No, Robert. I love An, and my father loved him. Our foolishness in Paris caused a great problem for our family."

"So, that's what we had in Paris, 'foolishness'?"

"Getting pregnant, especially at that time, was foolish."

"I never thought of it that way."

"Of course. You are a man, you would not."

"It has nothing to do with my being a man. You should have told me."

"To what end? I placed him in an orphanage and soon after married Bertrand, who had agreed to adopt him. He was a French solider at the time. We told An that his real mother was a hero of the party who died in an American air attack. This gave me and my father cover."

"And his real father? What did you tell him about his father?"

"That he was unknown. In time, the world came to think of Bertrand as the father since there was a resemblance."

"You lied to our son as a cover? And you kept this from me…"

"I could not tell you. And if I had, what would you have done? Move here? In the middle of a war between our countries?"

Robert crossed his arms over his chest. "Damn it, you still should have found a way!"

My Hanh moved closer to him. "In Vietnamese, the word *An* means 'peace.' This was for you. You used to care about peace," she whispered.

They continued walking in silence, side by side, passing by runners, bikers, and people on skates. The sun rose and the light shimmered across the lake. My Hanh spoke about An.

"He was a difficult child, often in trouble at school. He had a hard time focusing in class. He broke the rules, didn't get along with the other students. Many times, I used my father's influence to prevent his being expelled."

"He needed a father."

"He had a father. Bertrand has been good to him—and to me."

"He needed his *real* father!" Robert could no longer restrain his anger.

"To An, Bertrand *is* a real father."

He lowered his voice and spoke harshly. "How could you not tell him about me?"

"It was a choice, but it was the only choice," she said.

"Maybe for you, but look what you denied me, and our son!"

"The heartache of knowing he was half American?"

"You were selfish!"

Now My Hanh stopped again and abandoned her even temper, throwing up a boundary in her tone that warned Robert not to continue. "I made the choices I thought were best. Our culture, our politics have limits. If you disagree, fine. It's your right. But do not invalidate mine."

"Where is this restaurant?"

"Over there." She pointed across the street at the Luc Thuy Restaurant, a white, two-story, art deco building.

"I'm going to tell him I'm his father."

"You cannot."

"I will. I must."

"Robert, I invited you this morning to renew our friendship, not to make an enemy."

He looked at her and saw not only her insistence but a sadness as well. It moved him.

"I don't know what's right here." These were words that rarely if ever fell from his lips.

"So, you won't?" My Hanh softened her tone.

"He's my son, too, a son who doesn't know where he came from, a son whose past has been stolen—you stole it—and without it, he will lose his future, too."

"In Vietnam, family is the connecting tissue of life. You cannot tear it apart without risking grave danger. The moment you seek—to tell him the truth—may come, but it requires time and patience. It is not for now," My Hanh said. "So, please…"

Robert looked down to gather his thoughts, then lifted his head back up. "It's a lot to ask, My Hanh, but no, I won't—at least, not now."

No way I'm going to give up on my son. I will show him the loyalty my father did not show to me.

"Thank you, Robert."

They crossed the street, entered the restaurant, and found An sitting at a table eating *pho ga*, a traditional Vietnamese noodle soup. His head was buried in his bowl. He shoveled vegetables and slices of chicken into his mouth with his chopsticks and hardly paused to acknowledge the two of them standing over him.

"You could have waited for us!" My Hanh said, signaling the waiter to bring two more bowls.

"I was hungry!" An said as he dipped his chopsticks back into the soup.

Awkward pause. Robert stood silently. *God, he's just like me. I would have done the same.*

"This is my friend from Paris, Robert Samberg. You met him yesterday."

"I remember. . .the capitalist with the monopoly of American radio stations."

"Well, almost," Robert said.

He and My Hanh sat down. He studied An's face—straight black hair, green eyes, small nose, wide cheekbones, clear skin, the sum of a racial mix more handsome than its parts, nothing to signal American genetics instead of French. *How helpful for the charade!*

An looked away, laying down the chopsticks and picking up his spoon to eat the broth. Robert began tapping the table with the forefinger of his right hand. "In America, we call that chicken noodle soup." No response.

"Are you nervous about something?" An asked snarkily.

"Why do you say that?"

"You're tapping."

"Oh, it's just a habit of mine. It means nothing."

"An is a student at Science Po. He's returning to Paris the day after tomorrow," My Hanh said. "Robert and I met in Paris."

"I know, My Hanh, you told me—in '68."

Robert looked at her, surprised that An called her by her first name.

Must be his American genes. Vietnamese don't do that. He's angry.

"How do you like Paris?" Robert asked in a soft, break-the-ice manner.

"It's where my father is from. I feel at home there."

"At home, yes, well..." Robert struggled to find the right words.

"Paris is like that," My Hanh jumped in. "Over time it becomes part of you."

An looked quizzically at Robert. "My Hanh said you were a leader in the '68 student uprising." His tone had turned judgmental. "How did you become a capitalist?"

"I grew up," Robert responded flatly.

"Those of us who believe in revolution are not grown-ups?"

"No, I don't think they are."

"That's typical thinking for an American bourgeois elitist."

"An, Robert is our guest. We don't speak to our guests that way!" My Hanh leaned over the table to emphasize her point. The waiter arrived with the two additional orders of *pho ga*, placing the steaming bowls in front of Robert and My Hanh.

An was undeterred. "Look around you. There's nobody in this restaurant who did not lose family or a friend to the bombs your Air Force dropped!"

"An! Stop!"

"You're blaming me for the war?" Robert asked, his own tone now sharpening.

"Collective responsibility! Yes, I blame every American!"

"I opposed the war. Ask your mother."

"My *step*mother." My Hanh looked pained.

"You didn't do enough." An continued the attack.

"How do you know?" Robert asked.

"I know because the bombing didn't stop until we defeated you in 1975."

"I did what I could. Wars are fueled by passions and politics that are hard to contain. They take on a life of their own, a tragic momentum," Robert said.

"That's your excuse?"

"America has changed since then. We learned our limits."

"Limits? Who are you kidding?" An was not finished. My Hanh no longer tried to restrain him.

"No, I think America *has* changed," Robert reasoned.

"Ah, your bullshit incrementalism, your rhetorical progressivism. . .your elitist nonsense, all crap!" An said.

"I think you're being unfair. You're tarring and feathering all of us, while some of us, many of us, don't deserve it."

"To me, there are only two categories of Americans, those who pulled the trigger and those who enabled the trigger to be pulled," An said.

"What about the antiwar movement?"

"They failed—didn't go far enough, Sunday afternoon revolutionaries."

"Tell that to the four who died at Kent State," Robert said.

"What America needs is the destruction of your delusional, bourgeois sense of superiority and pseudo benevolence. Why are you here?"

"I was invited by the government to consult with the executives at Voice of Vietnam."

"So you can advise them to privatize and bring your reactionary, Western ideas to our people!" An said, bug-eyed.

"No. That's not on my agenda."

"The only way to fix America is to bridge the gap between the rich and poor through revolutionary struggle. Read Trotsky! Put that on your *agenda.* He had it right!"

"Trotsky?" Robert asked in mock ignorance.

"You don't know Trotsky?"

"Lev Davidovich Bronstein," Robert said mischievously.

"Okay, I'm impressed. Not many Americans know his name. How do you—"

"I read history—a ton of it, especially about nice Jewish boys who become iconic revolutionaries."

"What about Chairman Mao?" An asked.

"Mao Zedong, born in 1893…in Shaoshan village… an avid reader, admired strong emperors, loved reading historical novels, especially about rebellions and military heroes, admired George Washington."

"Someday, America will have a cultural revolution like China," An countered.

"I'm glad you have that figured out." *I want to reach this kid but I'm striking out.*

"Those left behind will stand up and march for what the elites never gave them—an equal playing field, power, prosperity." An's voice was steady and certain.

"Come on! Do your homework! America is about upward mobility! It's our strength."

"Used to be. No more. Your so-called middle class is in trouble, drowning in debt, fighting to tread water in an economic system that serves the few and stifles the many," An boldly proclaimed.

Robert grew more exasperated. "Is this what they teach you at Science Po?"

"No, but it's what I've figured out. I learn by opening my eyes, listening to my friends."

"You're hanging out with the wrong crowd." Robert glanced at My Hanh, who offered a sympathetic look but refused to be drawn into the battle. *Does she agree with this bullshit?*

"My best friends are from the Middle East. They have told me what your foreign policy has done to Muslims," An said accusingly.

"Enlighten me, An." *Here we go!*

"All America cares about is gorging itself on Arab oil."

"Hey, we don't steal it; we buy it; we pay for it!"

"America and the West destroyed the great culture of Islam, societies based on shariah law. You deny the legitimate aspirations of the Palestinians; you enable Israel to operate an apartheid state." An looked at Robert with contempt.

"Careful, man, you're talking to a Jew! I have zero tolerance for anti-Semitism."

"A Jew and a capitalist! Defender of a system rigged by the few who are rich, while the many who are poor are fed bullshit about so-called upward mobility." Robert's blood pressure was rising... *this kid is off the rails, nuts.* He again appealed to My Hanh, who again offered no support.

I give up! Robert paused to gather his thoughts. "Does your father know you think this way?"

My Hanh cocked her head and cast Robert a look to shut him down. "Robert, I think it best you leave Bertrand out of this."

"My father is a communist, a diplomat. He understands these things," An said, ignoring My Hanh.

"You need to take an American history class when you get to Paris. Your ideas are bullshit," Robert said.

"I've had enough!" An pounded the table. He rose from his chair, stormed out of the restaurant, jumped on his bike, and raced away.

"You were rough on him," My Hanh said, as she shook her head, looking upset and a little sad. She lowered her head, looked down at the bowls of *pho ga* getting cold on the table. They had stopped eating some time ago.

"He was rough on *me!*" Robert said bitterly.

"He's a bright boy with strong opinions—like you used to be."

"I was never like that— I don't agree with a word he says."

"Fathers and sons don't have to agree."

I've had enough father and son warfare for one lifetime! "I suppose you agree with him."

"Mostly, yes, but age and experience have taken off the sharp edges."

"I survive with my sharp edges," Robert said roguishly.

My Hanh nodded her understanding. "The weapons of success in capitalism."

How would she know? "The time change is killing me. I haven't stopped since I got here."

"We can go," she said in a voice that was slightly submissive.

"I could have used a little more support from you," he complained.

"How's that?" She reached to pull out her braids and smoothed her shimmering long black hair as it fell below her shoulders.

"I don't know. I was trying to reach our son and you were silent."

He looked at her face, now framed on both sides, projecting a glow forward like a beam of light. *God, she's still so beautiful!*

"Sometimes silence works better than words. An is young and radical, as you once were. Remember?" My Hanh asked, her voice soft, her manner full of life. She reached up and stroked her hair.

"And you are just as beautiful as you were back then." The words suddenly poured from him unfiltered. "Your hair is lovely when it's down, and your eyes—"

"Robert, please, that moment is gone. Everything is different now," she said firmly.

"Yes, our lives have changed. But when I look at you, I'm pulled back and I don't care about what's different. My feelings are the same," he said, his voice steady, his hands flat on the table.

"Robert, I think it's time to go."

"I need to ask you something." *Dangerous territory.*

"What?"

"For you, is there anything left between us? I mean do you—"

"Robert, I think those sharp edges are gone as well. Life has dulled them." She sat up, speaking directly but with a hint of melancholy in her voice.

"It's just that—well, for all these years, I never forgot."

"Robert, don't—"

"I'm sorry. We're both married and—I don't know—I just can't forget...the day I read your letter in the Jardin de Tuileries, under the oak tree, our special place. I had hoped we could stay together. I wanted to marry you, raise our child. I bought a ring. When I read that your father sent you home and our child wouldn't be born..." He felt vulnerable, out on an emotional limb, unfamiliar territory.

"Robert, I need to tell you the truth. My father didn't send me home." My Hanh's eyes were downcast. "I decided to leave. I wanted to accomplish things for my country and my career that were more important than our relationship or the pregnancy." She lifted her head and looked him in the eye, shamefaced. "You need to stop all this—"

"What are you saying?" Robert could feel his affection shriveling, collapsing.

"I lied in the letter as a cover." She kept her eyes on his.

"You...lied?"

"I reached for my dream, the dream of liberation, the dream of showing that a woman can be as strong as a man, the dream I have for all Vietnamese women. I had to leave. It was the only way," My Hanh said intensely.

"The only way?"

"Yes, the only way."

"And what about me? What about us? You ran home, had our son, and didn't tell me for twenty-two years! Hell, I still wouldn't know if I hadn't come for the exchange program. Your dream? What about *my* dream? Who the hell do you think you are? What kind of wom—"

"Don't put this all on me. You made choices, too. You married and you could have had other children. What about your wife?" My Hanh asked.

"She doesn't want children. She never had an interest in starting a family. She's more my business partner than my—"

"I see. I'm sorry."

Robert stood up, signaled the waiter to bring the check, and tossed a wad of 10,000-Dong notes on the table. He felt devastated. "Let's go."

"Yes," she responded as she rose too.

For a moment, the two of them looked at one another in silence as the tumult of the restaurant scene continued unabated—waiters hurrying to deliver plates of steaming food, patrons talking, laughing, some quietly, others out loud, couples sharing food, telling stories. Their silence muted everything around them. It was a shared space where each tried in vain to understand what had just happened, where they stood, how far it was from where they once had been—a moment of reckoning with an unknown outcome.

Robert decided to walk back to the hotel. My Hanh needed to take a rickshaw to make an appointment later that day. He walked her to the street and watched as she climbed into the rickshaw. "I would like see you again," he said, his anger diminished, his voice pleading.

"You will. Soon," she said as she gave her address to the driver and the rickshaw pulled away.

When Robert arrived at the hotel, the porter at the front desk handed him a message. The first negotiating session was set for the next morning at 7:00 at the Ngoc Son Temple on Jade Island. A small map and diagram showed the way. He walked to the suite, struggled to open the door with his key, went straight to the minibar, opened all three of the tiny Dewar's bottles in the refrigerator, gulped them, and picked up the phone to order three more.

Another night with little sleep.

Chapter 5

The next morning, sunlight streamed into Robert's room. He was still in the easy chair, his empty glass and the six tiny Dewar's bottles on the floor beside him. He spotted his grey suit, cleaned, pressed and wrapped in plastic hanging on a hook on the back side of the room door. A porter must have left it while he dozed. He rose, stretched, and took an extra-long cold shower.

Was I too honest, not honest enough? My Hanh, my first love. An, my son. She lied about leaving me and about An. He despises me. Am I a fool to think I can fix what's so broken? Undo the damage of time and events. Best to focus on the job at hand. Get the work done for Allen. Find out what they want. Save the acquisition and get home.

He skipped breakfast and cleared his head with two double espressos before putting on the suit and heading downstairs to hail a rickshaw for the short ride to the Ngoc Son Temple. He carried his leather attaché case filled with the briefing papers provided by the State Department and the note, map, and diagram delivered the night before. The city around him bustled with activity. A few years before, Vietnam had introduced reforms to allow the practice of "private capitalism," giving birth to many small businesses. As the rickshaw sped through the crowded streets, Robert saw colorful, hand-painted signboards announcing the openings of hair salons, restaurants and bars. He imagined these same streets in the bygone eras of colonial occupation by the Chinese, the French, the Japanese. He wondered if thunderous blasts from falling bombs were heard here in 1972, when America's Air Force dropped 20,000 tons of high explosives on Hanoi and Haiphong, killing 1,600 civilians. *The history here screams at you!*

The rickshaw arrived at the bright red Thê Húc Bridge, which stretched across the shimmering surface of Hoan Kiem Lake, which, like a red silk ribbon winding its way through a thick patch of willow and banyan tree branches, connected the noisy street to Robert's destination, the Ngoc Son Temple on Jade Island. He walked across the bridge, felt the soft breeze on his face, and smelled incense lit by a small group of visitors who prayed at the entrance to the temple. Following instructions on the map and diagram, he entered the building through one of the tall scarlet doors, passed a giant soft-shell turtle taxidermized and mounted in a glass case, and located a red lacquer-painted panel door behind the altar. He approached it carefully and, as instructed, knocked three times. When no one responded, Robert cautiously slid open the door and stepped into a dimly lit chamber with a low, beamed ceiling and colorful, flickering lanterns. The smell of incense infused the room. At its center was a long wooden table adorned with gold inlays, hand-painted flowers, and intricately carved legs. Behind the table stood the tall, imposing figure of a woman dressed in a striking blue and white áo dài, the candlelight illuminating her face.

"You!" Robert exclaimed and walked toward My Hanh, still angry but feeling awkward about having shared his feelings so honestly. *Working with her is going to complicate the hell out of this. How do you make peace with someone you don't trust...with a woman like that?*

"Me!" She held back the smile she might normally have offered. She was ready for business. "Please sit down, Robert." She motioned to a carved wooden chair across from her. An aide offered him an herbal tea that he did not want but accepted, taking a sip and holding back his grimace at the bitter taste. He pulled the briefing papers, each marked with a red, circular top-secret stamp, from the attaché case and placed them on the table before him.

"My mission is to find out what it will take to end the state of war between us. I'll be honest with you, there's nothing altruistic about this. Our government is concerned about China, their expansion in the South China Sea, or the East Sea as you call it. These briefing papers tell me there are those in your government who share that concern after the past ten years of border wars. We also know that some in your government have concluded that movement to a market economy and away from the command model of communism is a better way to go. We agree. We see opportunities for both our countries with outside investment and private-sector competition. Of course, there are some issues, and that's what we need to talk about, too. The biggest one on our side is getting back the remains of our fallen soldiers. We'll need that first. Nothing can happen without that. There's also the issue of your troops in Cambodia. The human rights issue. We've got big differences."

He paused, reached for his briefing papers, and looked up at My Hanh, who sat perfectly still and listened attentively. He waited for a response.

After a few moments of awkward silence, she leaned across the table. "Let me tell you a story. Five hundred years ago, when China's Ming Dynasty invaded Vietnam, a poor fisherman found a magical sword and brought it to our emperor, Le Loi, who used it to defeat the Ming army. When the peace was made and Le Loi was crossing this very lake on a boat, a giant turtle appeared at the surface and spoke to him. The turtle asked the emperor to return the sword. 'The world can only know peace if people let go of their weapons,' the turtle said. Amazed, the emperor took off the sword and placed it in the mouth of the turtle, which descended into the deep. From that day, this lake became known as Hoan Kiem—the Lake of the Returned Sword."

"A nice fairy tale," Robert said. "But..."

"The descendants of the turtle might say, 'The world can only know peace if people let go of their anger,'" she said, looking Robert in the eye.

"Look, about yesterday, I still don't—"

"Making peace also means letting go of the past...for our nations—and for us," she added. "That's how we'll be set free."

He looked down, pursed his lips, and said, "We've got some complicated issues to address and you're telling me fairy tales, like a woman tells a child..."

"Robert, legends are more than fairy tales; they are stories about wisdom, if we seek it. And Vietnamese women do more than raise their children and tell stories, much more."

He reached again for his briefing papers. "Can we please get started, now?"

"Yesterday, you asked what kind of woman I am?"

"I remember."

"Let me show you." She reached down to her briefcase and pulled out a sheaf of old photos of young female soldiers. Holding up the first photo of a young woman with binoculars, she said, "I am a woman like La Thi Tam, heroine of the People's Army, who risked her life to defuse powerful bombs during the American War." She lay the photo down and held up another of a different female soldier. "A woman like Pham Thi Binh who stood bravely at the target points of air attacks at the battle of Khe Sanh." My Hanh picked up the pace, raising and tossing each new female soldier's photo with increasing force to make her point. "Like Nguyen Thi Hanh, who drove trucks with supplies into raging battles, like Hoa Loc, Dong Phuong Hong, and Ngu Thuy, heroes of the Popular Armed Forces, who ran factories, nursed the wounded, repaired bomb damage, and shot down twenty-eight American warplanes."

The photos lay askew in front of Robert. "Is that your idea of returning the sword?"

"It's my idea of showing you the women of Vietnam, the mightiness underneath our gentleness, the cleverness underneath our modesty."

"Alright. I get your point," he said.

"What else did your CIA analysts put in those briefing papers?" She pointed to the stack in front of him.

"They wrote about another woman who reminded me more of you."

"Who is that?" My Hanh asked, surprised.

Robert rifled through the papers and held one up. "Nguyễn Thị Bình, a member of the Central Committee. This report says she is in line to become your Vice President."

"They did their homework. She is my mentor. When you and I met in Paris in '68, she was there. She worked closely with my father. She was our first female government minister."

"Another heroine?"

"Yes, very much."

"Can we talk now about reconciliation?" Robert smiled, realizing his question was a *double entendre*. This time, My Hanh returned the smile.

"You know, Robert," she said and leaned across the table again, "my father saw something special in you, 'a light in your eyes,' he would say—a light he never forgot even as the years passed."

"So that's why—"

"Yes, that's why he wanted you to speak at his ceremony, and it's why he wanted you to be here today."

"So can we get started? Will your government help us find the remains of our soldiers?"

"Well, let's see…according to our records, you lost 58,220 soldiers with 2,600 missing and about 150,000 wounded."

"That's right," he said.

"Robert, your military killed more than a million of our soldiers and two million of our civilians. Not to mention the lingering sickness and death from Agent Orange, the accidental deaths from unexploded ordinance—more bombs dropped on us than your Air Forced dropped in all the theaters of World War II. And the environmental devastation. How do we reconcile that?"

"There was killing and destruction on both sides…"

"The scale, Robert. There's no comparison, no moral equivalence. Your nation invaded ours." My Hanh spoke calmly but sternly. "We had a right to our defense just as we had a right to self-determination, unification, and independence."

"I think we should start from where we are now, not from where we were yesterday."

My Hanh looked at his finger tapping the table. "So where are we now?"

He did not hesitate. "Two nations, two ideologies at odds, not long ago locked in a bitter war, but today with common interests." He stopped tapping and pointed at the flowers painted on top of the table.

"We need to take small steps together—steps that will bloom like these."

"They are purple hyacinth, symbols of sorrow and regret. Given the massive destruction, the incomprehensible pain and suffering America brought upon us, I think an expression of regret is a good starting point to let go of the anger," My Hanh said. "They are beautiful, aren't they?"

"Our government didn't send me here to apologize. There are a lot of people in our government, a conservative, Republican government, who would not be happy if they knew what I was sent here to do. That was made clear to me. They would be even unhappier if I officially apologized."

"To apologize is to plow the field of dead seeds, old ways of thinking and to prepare the soil for a new and better harvest. That's how we grow trust. That's how we move forward."

"We are not farmers," Robert said.

"Washington, Jefferson, Adams—they were all farmers," she responded instantly. "America did massive damage to our people, our ecology and economy. You don't regret that?" she asked, casting him a look that said, *How could you not?*

She paused for effect.

"You're talking like our son," Robert responded, lowering his voice as if there might be someone listening. He whispered, "Our son, who doesn't know you're his mother and I'm his father!" He shook his head, his frustration mounting, his fatigue working against him.

"I see that you are having a problem letting go. You're asking our people to let the tragedy go, but you will not do the same with our past, you and I?"

"*I'm* having a problem?" he said, raising his voice and enunciating the statement as a question. "Why don't you apologize for lying to me about why you left Paris and to our son for lying to him about me?"

"Robert, I told you yesterday. I married. I have a husband. An has a father. Maybe I made a mistake lying to you about why I returned home from Paris. I was young and that was thoughtless. I'm sorry."

"I don't accept your apology."

My Hanh frowned and looked at him. "I told my father it might be too soon for this—he counted on your light. I see darkness," she said forcefully.

"My Hanh!" he snapped, exasperated.

"What do you want, Robert?"

"I want to get something done here—find our way to a new beginning."

"Such as?"

"Our missing in action...help us find them and bring them home."

"And if we do that?"

"We'll lift the trade embargo. This will bring prosperity."

"So we can become more like America?"

"What do you mean?"

"Your nation worships money and success. Your religion is the gross national product."

"What's wrong with a higher standard of living?"

"Nothing, except when that's all you're about. There's also the pursuit of happiness, in your Declaration of Independence. The man I see before me hides his unhappiness behind his possessions."

Robert tapped the table again, harder this time. "You're making this difficult."

"It's not my job to make it easy!"

This is going nowhere! Robert rose from his chair, cast a look of frustration, then paused and sat back down.

My Hanh reached over and placed her hand over his, interrupting his manic tapping. For a moment, there was silence as they felt each other's touch, and she kept her hand gently over his.

"Do you remember our Sunday mornings in Paris at Café Procope?" Robert asked, pulling his hand from under hers and placing it on top.

"Yes—we solved all the world's problems." She smiled.

"Can we please go back there?" he asked boyishly.

"One day, when I am elected chair—"

"The first woman. I will be proud of you."

"Will you?" My Hanh looked at him, wide-eyed.

"If we do something constructive here, it might help you get there.".

"Yes, it might."

My Hanh pulled back her hand, reached for the photos of the female soldiers still on the table in front of Robert, and returned them to her briefcase.

"What if we started with an office here in Hanoi to coordinate the search for our missing in action?"

"We must include reparations and assistance to repair environmental damage," My Hanh insisted.

"I can sell that. It's a small price for the bigger prize Secretary Baker wants, checking the advance of China."

"You Americans never stop thinking of your 'big picture,' and the rest of us are just pawns in your game."

"That's why I got away from public service. The Muslim who shot Robert Kennedy killed something in me, too," Robert said.

"You should have told that to An yesterday."

"I don't think he would have understood."

"What's wrong?"

"I'm thinking about how hard it will be to reach him, maybe impossible."

"It will take time," she said. "He's young. He doesn't know you. He doesn't know you love him."

"But he hates me."

"He's angry and he hasn't yet learned to let go of it," she said.

"To return the sword..."

"When someone is angry, they are in pain. That's where you must look if you want to reach him. That's how you set them free."

"Why is there such conflict between fathers and sons?"

"Why do you say that?"

"Because I struggle with my father—it's a big problem."

My Hanh looked at Robert as if to invite him to continue. "Problem?"

"Before I came here, I found out the man who runs my father's company is challenging my radio purchase. It's a process that requires government approval."

"I see the pain and the worry on your face."

"Remember how I helped your father in Paris—met with him, spoke to him about the antiwar movement, helped him deliver a message to the White House?"

"Of course I remember."

"So you know the risk I took," he reminded her. "Nobody knew, and they still don't know how much—"

"That was long ago," she said, as if the risk were long over.

"The man filing against me, my father's protégé, is using this as evidence of disloyalty. He's falsely accusing me of being unpatriotic, unworthy of holding a broadcast license."

"My god, McCarthyism survives all these years later?" My Hanh asked.

"It does." Robert rubbed his eyes, the lack of sleep catching up with him.

"This man works for your father?" she said, a tone of incomprehension in her voice.

"When my father retired, he chose this man, Dick Dellmore, over me to run the family business. He broke his word to me, an act of disloyalty—to his son. I left and started my own company, built it to become the nation's largest—provided the acquisition is approved. Dellmore is trying to stop me." *A relief to share this with her.* "You know, the only other one I speak to about this is Macallan."

"A close friend?" she asked.

"My horse." He forced a smile, embarrassed by how odd it must sound to her. *Am I really that alone?*

My Hanh looked at him incredulously.

"It's complicated," Robert said as he shook his head and half chuckled, trying to make light of it.

"Like a son never told about his real father and mother?" she asked.

"Something like that." Then, he looked her in the eyes, finding common ground in their shared secrets.

"Why did you come here, Robert?"

"I would like you to think I came to return the sword, but that would be a lie."

"Why then?"

"I had no choice. The people who asked me to come have the power to help me win government approval for the purchase. They needed me. I needed them. It's that simple."

"You came for money, not for peace," she said.

"Yes, but there was another reason…"

"Me?"

"My memory of us. I told you it has never gone away. And now there is An…"

"You and your father, you and An, you and Dellmore—your life is filled with conflict."

"Isn't that part of life?"

"Yes, the struggle of opposites."

"Is that where *we* are?" Robert kept his eyes on hers.

"I don't know." She looked away.

"Right." He rose from his chair. "What more do you need from me?"

"Nothing," she responded and rose as well.

"Have we done enough?"

"There is a lot to let go, on both sides. It will take time," she said as she returned her eyes to his. "But there is a pathway forward, and I will report that to our chairman."

"And a pathway for us?"

"I don't think so, Robert," she said, haltingly.

"If I return my sword?" he implored.

She nodded, smiled, and whispered, "You are a brilliant salesman."

"The light?" he asked, then smiled back.

They walked together to the red-lacquered sliding door. Robert turned to My Hanh as if to a girl before a kiss on the first date, uncertain of what to do, unsure of her feelings, but clear in the realization that she was with him in a way he never could and perhaps never would completely understand. Against his better judgment, he still wanted her. They stood in silence at the door, shook hands, and said goodbye.

"Wait," she said suddenly. "I almost forgot."

"What?"

She reached into her briefcase and pulled out a photo of An taken when he was a young boy in Bac Son Valley. "It's from my father's mantel at the house. He would have wanted you to have it."

"Thank you." He nodded and walked through the door, head down, his briefcase in one hand, and the photo of An in the other.

When he'd arrived in Vietnam, he thought he would do the mission and return home quickly to the life he had known. Now the ground of that life trembled beneath him—a lost love re-ignited, a son to love who rejected him, an idea about peace planted within him, not in the political sphere, which he understood, but in the heart, which he did not. His mission was over. He would be leaving Vietnam, but Vietnam would not be leaving him. Like an early morning mist before sunrise, it would linger, its mysteries, its legends embedded and destined to return. Before this visit, his life was about getting ahead or getting even, and now, for the first time, he began to think about letting go—truly returning the sword. This was a sea change. His head reeled from it. He would carry it home.

Chapter 6

Robert soaked, eyes closed, listening to the seagulls and the crashing waves in the elevated, custom-built hot tub in his bedroom—98 massage jets, audio system, waterfall, and an adjoining ice tub. A bank of hidden microphones picked up the sounds of the Atlantic Ocean just outside. He opened his eyes. A wall of glass gave him an unobstructed view of the beach. It had been a tough few weeks since his return from Vietnam. He had worked at headquarters in New York City, and this was his first day back in Palm Beach. The events of the day raced across his mind, but memories of his secret mission lingered as well. He switched off the sounds of the ocean and searched for the signal of his new radio station in New York. A satellite link enabled him to pick up any major market station in the country.

His home on Palm Beach was a showcase of luxury and technology. It had been featured in *Architectural Digest*. The reporter marveled at the secret door in the bedroom, camouflaged by a wall of mirrors, leading directly to the beach that enabled Robert to sneak special guests into the room undetected. Andi slept in a separate bedroom as their schedules and sleep patterns differed. She snored and he was a light sleeper. They lived separate lives, together, something that before his mission to Vietnam he never gave a second thought but that now felt amiss, empty.

Once home, he threw himself into his work—to complete the acquisition and defend against the license challenge—a convenient distraction from troubling thoughts about My Hanh and An. This was no easy task. There were new radio stations to assess—format, management, talent, and marketing—and the applications at the Federal Communications

Commission (FCC) with everything at risk because of Dellmore.

Robert's money bought him the best help. He hired the nation's leading communications law firm, Arent, Fox and Stone, to represent him at the FCC. He gave them carte blanche, "anything you need." He knew that the Dellmore challenge, which raised questions about his loyalty to America, could become an insurmountable obstacle. He knew that any evidence presented that he had aided Thành in Paris in 1968 could be twisted to paint him as disloyal no matter his motives, no matter the truth.

Hysteria over communist affiliations in 1990 was not as toxic as it had been in the 1950s, but it was still considered political poison among right-wing politicians and pundits. Robert prepared for a bare-knuckle street fight. He hired Washington's largest private investigation firm, Moya and Moya, to follow Dellmore and scour his background for dirt. He demanded they submit weekly reports on the man's habits, movements, the people he met, even his golf scores. But there was only one piece of information they uncovered that threw him.

"Andi! Goddammit!" Robert had stomped out onto the wraparound balcony at his oceanside estate at sunset that evening, clutching the report from Moya. "You're screwing Dellmore's new attorney!" He hadn't bothered to buckle his pants, which were half off and falling to his knees. "Moya has Slate bragging about you to Dellmore on a phone tap. How could you be so stupid!"

"Robert, I'm sorry! I didn't know Jack was working for Dellmore." Jack was Jack Slate, lead partner at Slate and Stern whom Andi had met at a Rotary fundraiser at the Breakers Hotel. She looked shaken, her pink Lily Pulitzer beach cover flapping in the breeze. She had just taken a dip in the ocean as was her custom on summer evenings. "I didn't know, I—I was lonely. He showered me with attention."

"The diamonds, the Mercedes, this house. I don't shower you with enough attention?" Robert buckled his pants as he paced back and forth along the deck to douse the flames of his anger and his nervous energy. Their marriage felt loveless to him, but he had fooled himself into believing it was something more for her. *It's okay for husbands to wander, not for wives.*

"Robert, it's not about *things*—it's something else."

"What then? Why don't you just tell me? I'm not a mind reader." He shot his words at her as if from a high-powered rifle, then turned away. *With Dellmore's attorney of all people!*

"Your heart is somewhere else! I've felt it for years."

Robert did not respond. *Does she know?*

"Your affairs—the women who come and go—I couldn't bear it anymore."

"Yeah, tough life!" He waved his arms at the view of the ocean illuminated by the moonlight.

"I'm lonely! Jack gives me the affection I never get from you."

Robert squinted. "You're lying—you must have known." He was in hard, cold, take-no-prisoners mode. "You're helping him."

"Robert, I cheated in the marriage, just like you, but not in the business. I have been unfaithful, but not disloyal to the firm."

"Your lover represents the motherfucker who is painting me as a communist sympathizer because I helped Thành stop a war twenty-two years ago. They're trying to sink our deal."

"Robert, we're both on the company loan guarantees; if we don't get approved, we're both screwed. I swear I didn't know. Jack never told me."

"Well, now you know!" *You just had to do this to me, didn't you?*

"Robert, you don't plan things like this, they just happen. Besides, it's not Dellmore, it's your father. Dick can't be doing this without your father's blessing."

He looked away. *She's right. It's my fucking father. He hurt me as a boy, he hurt me as a young man, he's still trying to hurt me.* "Well, they don't just happen to me!" His eyes blazed. The mention of his father had stoked his anger. He grabbed a black iron fire poker from the fire pit and slammed the top rail surrounding the deck. Andi blanched. His rage scared even himself. He tossed it back down.

"Robert—we can deal with this." She reached out in a gesture of peace. He motioned for her to back away. The two stood silently a few feet apart, which, in the moment, felt like a few miles. They faced the ocean, watching the light of the full moon reflecting on the water.

"Jack doesn't know that I know. That could be useful." Robert defaulted to scheming mode, his mood lightening a bit.

"What are you saying?"

"Sleep with the slimeball if you must, but not a word about the business, not a word about the FCC...except for what I tell you to feed him." He spoke in the authoritative manner he used at work, his voice steady and strong.

"Understood." Andi nodded to him as she had on countless occasions when brainstorming sensitive business issues.

The ground broken, she switched gears, her concern genuine. "Robert, you haven't been yourself since you returned from Vietnam. You seem distracted, and the staff has noticed."

"I'm trying to sort out some things."

"What things?"

"Dellmore, my father, the shitstorm we're in..."

"It's a lot," she said.

"I've been fighting so long and so hard. Someone punches me, I punch back harder. It's what I've learned—"

"To survive. It takes a warrior to survive in this business."

"Last week, when we met with the morning man at WNGS and he told us about his son's illness, I cut him off. His boy is going to die, and I dove right back into the ratings."

Andi looked him, somewhat startled. "You're running a business, Robert, not a therapy session."

He picked up the fire poker and put it back in its holder. "Yeah, I'm good at that, aren't I?"

"Robert, with everything going on, you need to get it together."

"Your affair sure as hell isn't making things any easier." He paused, picking up the half-empty glass of scotch and soda she had left on the deck table just beside them. He looked at her and softened. *We've been here before.* "Want a refill?" She nodded. "Did you send my report on the meeting in Hanoi to Hoffers?"

"I sent it out yesterday."

"Did you destroy the notes and erase the file?"

"Yes, sir."

"That stuff is secret. You can't talk about it."

"Speaking of Hanoi...how was it seeing My Hanh?" Andi knew about Robert's past.

"Like going to a twenty-year class reunion. Everybody's older and chubbier. You hardly recognize the faces, and you don't know them anymore."

"How was it, really?" Andi said.

He would never admit how unsettling it was. "She's married. She's not the same."

"You're married, and you're not the same, either."

"No, I'm not." Robert looked away, feeling hollow. *Haunted by a lover and a son...and a damn turtle! Let go of my weapons, my anger? And lose? What light? I'm in the dark where I belong, but I don't like it anymore.* He hid his distress as he often did by bragging. "Allen said I performed better than a career diplomat."

"I thought your recommendations made sense, especially setting up the office in Hanoi for the missing in action. I'll bet some good comes from it."

"Thanks," he said. He looked at Andi and saw in her face the young college girl he had met many years before. *She's right. My heart is elsewhere. And she has stayed by my side, many years. She screws up, but she is loyal and that counts. That counts.*

The next morning, Robert held a meeting with his legal team at the company's Florida office on the top floor of the Phillips Point building overlooking Lake Worth. The purpose was to review strategy at the FCC against Dellmore and his father's company, Samcom, which Dellmore ran as CEO. A secretary interrupted the meeting to hand over a note. There was a call for Robert from Paris. He stepped out of the room.

"My Hanh! What are you doing in Paris?" It had been a month since their meeting at Ngoc Son Temple on Jade Island.

"An is missing. He has not been seen at school for two weeks. The

Paris police can't find him. My contacts at our embassy can't find him."
Her tone was staccato, almost frantic. Her concern flooded him, too.

"I'm sorry. I really am."

"Do you think Allen Hoffers might help?"

"I don't know. There's a war brewing in Iraq. He has his hands full
right now."

"Too full to help our son?"

Her question rubbed Robert the wrong way. "*Our son?* You mean
your stepson and Bertrand's son!"

"Robert, please don't push me away. An needs your help. *I* need
your help. I'm asking you to be there for us."

"Christ, I've got Dellmore labeling me a commie at the FCC. I don't
need this!"

"I know that, Robert, but I've tried every—"

"Can't Bertrand help?"

"He's at the embassy in Kuwait. He contacted the head of the French
police. Nothing is working."

"Look, My Hanh, I'm in a meeting with my attorneys. It's almost
over. I'll have to call you back."

"Robert, please!"

"I'll get back to you. I will." He returned to the conference room,
flooded with emotion about the call. *My son is in danger. She's asking
me to help. If I do, and it gets out, it will play into Dellmore's hands. They'll
say I helped the communists in '68 and I'm still helping them! Shit!* The lawyers were standing around the table gathering their papers, getting
ready to leave. Robert motioned for them to sit back down. "We are at
war," he said in a low, authoritative voice, "and I want every weapon
deployed. I'm not going to lose this deal over what I did twenty-two
years ago. I helped Thành to jump-start peace talks that were being
illegally sabotaged. I had authorization. No matter how these assholes
try to distort it, my actions were patriotic, not treasonous. You guys
need to make that clear. You need to build me up and tear Dellmore
down. Use every means! We need to kick ass, everyone!"

The lawyers filed out of the room and Robert was left alone. The late morning sun poured through the windows. He adjusted the blinds to keep out the heat, then made himself a double scotch and stared at the boats passing in the intercoastal waters below. His eye caught a sailboat tacking hard in the distance. *Looks like a toy boat from here.* He thought about the day twenty-two years before when he and My Hanh had won a toy sailboat race in the great fountain in the Tuileries Garden, competing with a father and his young son. *What a win!* He recalled the pained look on the young boy's face—how the father had wrapped his arms around the boy, hugged and consoled him. It was as if they were both right there in the conference room, splashing the water, speaking in French, and holding each other in their moment of loss. *I've never had a hug like that from my own father. Never.*

"Oh, shit!" He slapped the button on the intercom. The receptionist responded. "Get me Allen Hoffers at State."

Chapter 7

Once again at the bar at the Hotel Crillon, Robert sipped his second glass of *Macallan 1926*, chatting with Pierre Le Rest. Pierre gazed at him, towering over him from behind the bar, stroking his ample mustache, weighing his next words.

"You look worried, my friend."

"I am," Robert said as he motioned for Pierre to refill his glass.

"It might help if you just tell me about it."

"Yeah, well, maybe later."

"Talk to me, Robert," Pierre said as he held his fist in front of Robert's face.

"My son is missing."

"A son?" Pierre looked incredulous. "You never told me."

"I didn't know."

"That he was missing...?"

"That I had a son."

"You're not making any sense."

"I know." Robert gulped the last drop of whiskey. "Another!"

My Hanh entered the room, a somber look on her face, dressed in a blue blazer, jeans, and a white silk shirt, carrying a grey leather bag, the strap falling over her right shoulder—a striking contrast to the outfits worn by the women Robert customarily met at the bar on his visits. She surveyed the row of stools until she spotted him, then walked over and sat down next to him.

Pierre looked up from wiping the bar just in front of her. "*Mon Dieu!*" He raised his long arms in the air, his apron strings unraveling, nearly falling to the floor. "My Hanh! *Incroyable!* I can't believe it!" He reached for her with the excitement of a schoolboy and said to Robert, "Why didn't you tell me?" He'd last seen her when he led the two of them on a midnight tour of the Catacombs of Paris in 1968.

"Hello, Pierre." My Hanh smiled and spoke as if twenty-two days, not twenty-two years had passed. She placed her right hand on his forearm and kissed him on both cheeks, stretching her tall, lean body across the bar. Robert watched the two of them transfixed, returning for a moment to the Paris of his youth, the Paris that had never left him.

"What can I get you?" Pierre asked.

"Perrier. I gave up alcohol," she said quietly as she turned to Robert. "I got your message and I'm grateful that you came." She leaned over to offer him kisses, French style, on both cheeks. He could smell her perfume as her lips smacked the air against his right, then his left cheek, his senses amplified by the effects of the *Macallan*.

Pierre left to serve a bearded man wearing a keffiyeh—traditional Arabic headgear—sitting nearby eyeing them. *A rich Arab spending our oil money. Why is he looking at us?* The two sat side by side, facing ahead, each sipping their drink. Robert broke the silence. "Look, I'm sorry I gave you a hard time on the phone."

"It's okay. You came. That's what counts."

"Thanks."

"First my father, now this…it's a sad time for me. Life is testing me."

"Allen set up a meeting in the morning at the American Embassy with Ambassador Tom Curley and CIA station chief Bill Brooks. They have access to electronic surveillance and other tools. If they're willing to use them, it will help you find An."

"Aren't you coming?" Her face registered disappointment and concern.

"I don't know. If I take this too far, it could come back to haunt me—I've got hearings coming up on the license challenge."

"But this is for your son." She looked pained.

"You told me in Hanoi that I've been hanging on to an illusion, a dream that's passed."

"That was about us, not about your son. His life may be at stake. I'll have no leverage tomorrow without you. I need you there."

"Maybe it's something innocent, a new girlfriend, a trip he didn't tell you about."

"Robert, my instincts are clear. He's in trouble. I don't know how bad, but I know it's not good."

"Is Bertrand coming?"

"Of course, he'll be there in the morning. He's traveling all night."

"A reliable man—"

"Yes, when I push him."

He shook his head. "Like you're pushing me...if this gets out—"

"Robert, think about your son, not about yourself."

"You didn't when you lied to him about me..."

"It's not the same," she said.

"It *is* the same. You put your needs above his."

"If you are exposed helping An, you can recover. A man has more options to recover than a woman."

"I think you're overestimating my power to recover from a right-wing attack that sinks a business deal I spent years to accomplish, and huge sums of money."

"You're underestimating how difficult it is for a Vietnamese woman to attain political power if it is known she is the mother of an American child."

"We both have our problems," he said.

"Right now, we have the same problem, our son."

"Yes...yes..."

"So you'll come?"

"I don't know."

"If you ever hope to reach him, you must."

"Your father once told me, 'If you have a son, you have a descendent, but you cannot say so even if you have ten daughters.'"

"I remember...it was the night we had dinner in this room."

"Did he really believe that?" Robert asked.

"Yes. That thinking was ingrained. It pained him each time I broke the mold of the traditional Vietnamese women, but eventually, he accepted me and supported my ambitions. He helped promote me to leadership in the party, and in our last conversation, he told me he was proud of me."

"You're lucky. I have never heard those words from my father."

"You're a son…it's easier to win respect than if you were a daughter."

"Not in my family. Once, my sisters Dottie and Lorraine decided to paint the back of our house. They thought it would look better red, and they asked me to help. So we found my father's paints in the garage and worked all afternoon until the entire back of the house was a shockingly bright red. He came home, was furious, and held a kangaroo court. They lied and said it was my idea. I defended myself, but I was the only one punished—smacked repeatedly on the butt with a paddleboard—while they got off scot-free."

"You're still angry about it?"

"I don't give up my anger as easily as your emperor, Le Loi," he said.

"You remember the story."

"Returning the sword? Yes, I think about that."

She smiled and looked at him. "You are a bundle of contradictions, Robert."

"I know…and you?"

"To be honest, ever since we met in Hanoi, I've been thinking, too—"

"That's dangerous," he said, trying unsuccessfully to be funny.

"I'm angry, too…angry that my political path is so hard because I'm a woman…angry that my marriage, like yours, is a business arrangement, and yes, angry that I felt forced to lie to our son and hide my love for him to protect my cover."

"You're forcing me to lie to him, too."

"I know, and I'm thinking we must find another way to deal with this. I don't know what way or when to do it, but…"

Robert put down his drink and turned to her. "So, we both have swords to return."

She nodded. Took the last sip of her Perrier. "You hide your pain with your possessions. I hide mine with the pursuit of power. The effect is the same. We're both alone."

"And isolated from our son," he added.

Her face fell. "We have harmed him."

Robert grunted, took a sip of his drink, and mumbled, "We? I would have liked the chance."

Perhaps for the first time, it seemed she saw the pain she had wrought and changed the subject. "You look tired. How was your flight?"

"A lot better than that night in '68 when I returned from Washington, ring in my pocket, and you stood me up, big time."

"Robert, are you ever going to let that go?"

"Why should I?" His resentment was unleashed again from the effects of the scotch.

"You know, this is hard for me, too." She turned toward him, leaning in. "It's hard to see you—hard to be here in Paris again. I just lost my father. My son is missing. I feel like a jumble of selves, the Vietnamese woman, the French woman of my marriage, and the lover who walked out on you long ago."

Robert was stunned. He froze, silent, then whispered, "If you loved me, why the hell did you leave me? I still don't understand."

My Hanh turned away, sat straight up on her barstool, and after a moment's pause, began to speak in a soft voice. "When I was a girl, I used to have this dream. There was a peasant girl, her face blurred, cooking dinner in a small kitchen. Her husband would enter the room, complain that the house was dirty, and scold her because she was cooking rice when he had asked for noodles. He was unemployed. She was the sole breadwinner for the family. She had just returned from a long day working in the fields. She ran the household, raised the children, and managed the family finances—like a good Vietnamese wife. In the dream, he would scream at her and slap her across the face. 'What kind of family is it when the wife does not obey her husband?' She winced and did not raise a hand or say a word in her own defense. Then, a single tear would run down her cheek, and at this point, I would awaken in a sweat, even on the coldest nights. Robert, I had this dream so many times, I came to believe that it was my karma to stand up for this peasant girl who would not, who *could* not stand up for herself—that in a former life, this girl paid the price so I could live my life free of male domination and pass the lesson to future generations."

"Your mission?"

"Yes, in 1968, I felt what you felt, and it frightened me because I thought those feelings meant I would become like the peasant girl in the dream. I could not let that happen. I had to follow a different path, *my* path."

Robert held the Glencairn goblet of *Macallan* the entire time My Hanh spoke and did not take another sip. "But you married!"

"Yes, I married. I told you. I had to—to protect my father, my family, and my career. Bertrand made a great sacrifice to protect my political future. Our marriage is—"

"What?"

"More a friendship, a partnership than a passion."

"My god. That's what I have with my wife, Andi."

"So, we are still two peas in the same pod?" she said, her words harkening back to the way they described their relationship in its halcyon days.

"Except my wife is having an affair—seems friendship and partnership aren't quite enough for her."

"How are you handling that?"

"I got angry. When I calmed down, I adjusted and used her betrayal for my own good. Her lover is an attorney for the company challenging the transfer of the radio stations."

"A wise man does not allow his emotions to get in the way of his decisions."

"And a wise woman the same," Robert added, savoring My Hanh's compliment.

"I'm happy to hear you say that. Successful women must spend a lifetime biting their tongues in the face of powerful, insensitive men."

"Except for when you walked out on me. Then, a man was gutted by an insensitive woman. You hollowed me out," he said, frowning.

"I'm sorry, Robert."

He put down his glass. He swallowed hard. His mood shifted in an instant. The whiskey loosened his tongue. "Sorry? You gave up on our love, traded something rare, something real, for an imitation, a fake—you settled, and blew it for both of us! For all your ambition and wisdom, you're a damn fool!"

"And you?" she asked, pausing. "With all your money, your fancy scotch and radio empire—with no one to share it with but a horse, your only friend? Who's the fool?"

"You have no fucking idea!" he roared.

"Men like you think you have a free reign and we women have to take it and suffer."

"You think Andi suffered? I *made* her! I gave her everything!"

"The everything you gave her I'm sure is nothing she didn't earn."

"And you would know this *how*?" he barked.

"When I left Paris, I thought it was the best thing for both of us. We were so young...our cultures so different...our countries enemies...I didn't think our relationship could go anywhere."

"Oh, bullshit! It was selfishness, naked ambition!" he said indignantly.

"No, Robert."

"Yes! You cut me out of the choice! Had our son and never told me!" He yelled and nearby patrons looked up. "Robbed me of becoming the father I always wanted to be and robbed An of the father he'll never have. Does that sound fair to you?"

Pierre heard the commotion, too, and returned to his old friends. "Are we okay here? The lady over there in the blue dress asked me to call security. The man at the table next to her in the keffiyeh is staring at you. I think you've upset him." He nodded in their direction.

My Hanh reached out and touched Pierre's hand. "Just a spat." She looked at Robert. "We'll tone it down."

Robert turned to his old friend Pierre. "Send a bottle of vintage Veuve to the lady, okay? And a Perrier to the Muslim."

"And please apologize," My Hanh added, casting a see-how-easy-that-was look at Robert.

Pierre gazed at the two for a moment, who once again sat side by side, looking straight ahead just as they were when he'd last left them. "Behave yourselves," he admonished them gently and, with a quizzical look, turned and departed.

Robert sat up on his stool, squirmed, and stretched. He looked at My Hanh and she at him. *We used to fall into each other's arms and make crazy love after an argument.* In the passion of their anger and the free flow of their emotions, the old juices flowed. Each breathed more deeply, processing the words and feelings of the other. *She still brings me to a place where I'm off guard, where my social mask is torn away by her truth, and no matter how unpleasant, I somehow feel alive with her, just the way it was before.* My Hanh rose from her stool. Robert jumped up, too, and took her hand. She did not resist, and their hands melded comfortably. They walked to the elevator in silence.

"Come up," he said, his invitation masked as a command, but offered in a soft voice, his heart pounding.

"No," she said, though the softness of her smile said differently.

"Come tomorrow," she shot back.

"For you, or for An?"

"For both of us. Come for both of us."

Robert entered the elevator alone, tapped the button for the top floor, and turned for one last look. He didn't say anything, but he saw in her look that she understood he would be there in the morning.

Chapter 8

The next morning, Robert rose early, ordered breakfast from room service, and dressed to walk across Avenue Gabriel, the narrow street that separated the Hotel Crillon from the Hôtel de Talleyrand, site of America's oldest diplomatic outpost abroad. As a student of history, he reveled in the fact that the earliest ambassadors to serve at this embassy—Franklin, Jefferson, Morris, Monroe, and Livingston—were founding fathers of the nation. He'd slept well and somehow felt better. Maybe it was his decision to attend the meeting, or maybe it was where he had left things with My Hanh the night before. *Returning the sword...for me, it's not so easy.*

He poured some coffee and sat at the mahogany desk with the antique-style phone in front of the French windows overlooking the Place de la Concorde, where in the 18th century men lost their heads on the guillotine. *Slicing off heads—gruesome! A perfect fate for Dellmore. Ugh! Better check in with Allen before the meeting.* He winced as he pulled out a card from his wallet with phone numbers, then asked the hotel operator for a long-distance line and dialed the number for Allen Hoffers in Washington.

He raised his voice. "Allen, it's Robert. I took your advice."

"So you decided to go," he responded. "Congratulations. You did a mitzvah."

"Yeah, not my usual style. I'm just having breakfast before heading to the meeting."

"Are you sure about going? Curley and Brooks can handle it. They're good at these things. I told them to offer full support to find An," he said. "You can stay in the background."

"Yeah, well, my life's already complicated. I thought I'd add to it—My Hanh wants me there."

"My Hanh wants...you...there?" Allen teased. "Sounds like more than a mitzvah. Careful!"

"Always!" he boasted. "How are things with you?"

"I'm up to my neck with stuff I can't talk about."

"Business as usual, huh?"

"Some worrisome chatter from the Middle East."

"Well, I'm safe. I'm in Paris. Did you read my report on the meeting in Hanoi?"

"Well done, my friend. I think there's a basis there to move things forward. It's in policy review."

"Anything new on the FCC license thing?"

"I had lunch with Duggen. He's a Bush appointee, a good man. He can't say what Dellmore submitted to justify the challenge, but he assured me you'll get a fair hearing."

"What about the letter from LBJ clearing me?"

"I've got a search underway at the FBI, the CIA, and the NSA. It also might be in the presidential papers at the LBJ Library in Austin. I sent someone there, too."

"Good, you're covering all the bases."

"Let me know what happens with your son," Allen said, yawning. It was past his bedtime.

"'My son'—I'm not used to hearing those words."

"I hope you find him."

"Me too. Thanks for your help, Allen."

He hung up the phone, looked out the window at the traffic in the Place de la Concorde, and poured himself a fresh cup of coffee. *I'm taking a risk to help reach my son. Should I take a risk to help reach my father? Give back the sword? He's got to be behind what Dellmore is doing. But why?* He picked up the phone, hesitated, took a breath, then dialed his father's private phone in Palm Beach. Irwin lived at an independent living facility not far from Robert's seaside mansion. Despite the proximity, they rarely saw one another or spoke. The phone rang and rang, and he waited, tapping the table with his index finger.

"Who is this?"

"It's Robert."

"Why the hell are you calling me in the middle of the night? You woke me!"

"Sorry, Irwin. . . I thought you might still be up. I'm in Paris."

"Oh, Paris—buying a bottle of whiskey that costs as much as a house?"

"No, not that." Robert gripped the phone tightly, his hand suddenly sweating.

"So, why *are* you calling?"

"I was just thinking of you, I mean, thinking that maybe we should sit down and talk when I get back," he said haltingly.

"About what?" Irwin asked, his tone brusque.

"I don't know—about how things have gone before and how they are going and maybe—"

"Robert, look, you don't have to. . . ."

"No, I just think there are some things we can go through. . .and I want to understand better." *I need to confront him about the challenge.*

"Well, I'm tired, need to go back to sleep. You know where I live. Call me when you get back."

It's never the right time. "Okay Dad."

"'Dad'? You never call me that. Something wrong?"

"No. Fine. Goodnight." Robert hung up as his breakfast arrived. *Damn, that was useless! I just can't talk to him.* A uniformed butler set the table and placed a basket of warm croissants and pastries before him. He refilled Robert's cup and turned to leave. Robert handed him a fifty Franc tip. *I better not let my guard down. I need to make sure Andi is on top of things at home.* He picked up the phone again.

"Hello," Andi said, her voice groggy from sleep.

Taking a sip of coffee, he asked, "You alone?"

"Yes, yes!" she said, sounding surprised to hear from him. And glad. "When are you coming back? There's a ton of work on the acquisition."

"Anything you can't handle?"

"No, I'm on top of it."

"I need you to let the Cantor Fitzgerald people know I'm here and will be out of touch for a couple of days. Also the guys from Deloitte—tell them I still need the numbers on all fifty stations. Wire them to the hotel. I need this no later than tomorrow, if you can handle it."

"Why do you always say that? You know I can," she said, her displeasure evident.

"Hey, it's just a turn of phrase," he assured her.

"Is it?" Andi asked, a pique in her voice.

"Anything new on Dellmore?"

"Jack doesn't mention him, and I don't ask. I don't want to seem pushy or prying."

"Tell Jack I'm vacationing in Paris, buying a bottle of wine that costs as much as an airplane." *That's sure to get back to dear old dad.* "I want the bastards to think I don't have a clue."

"Robert, what if he starts pumping me for information?"

"Don't tell him shit, or better yet, tell him how fragile things look, complain that our funding is still not solid, that we're not set up to handle the workload," he instructed. "Dribble it out one thing at a time, you know how to do that. Make him believe he's in a strong position and that we are weak."

"I understand." She spoke as if on a business call, but her tone telegraphed some regret. *I think she misses me.*

"Remember, we're soon going to be the largest broadcast firm in America!" he said as if he were trying to convince himself, too.

"What *are* you doing over there?"

"I told you, shopping for wine."

"Right...you're keeping things from me! Don't get yourself in trouble."

"Who gets in trouble in Paris?" he responded with a chuckle.

"Alright then." Something unspoken hung in the air.

"I need to hang up before my croissants get cold...the buttery ones, the good ones, remember?"

"I remember," she said wistfully.

"Goodbye, partner," he said. Calling her partner was his term of endearment. *I really do rely on her, don't I? God, I hate admitting that. I need to keep her happy.*

He hung up and gazed out the French window at the sun rising across the Place de la Concorde. He paused to savor the majestic view of the monumental fountains and the 3,300-year-old Obelisk of Luxor at the center of the Place. It was unseasonably cold and windy. The gusts captured the water rising from the fountains and sprayed the surrounding sidewalks. He reached for a croissant, smeared it with butter and strawberry preserves, and poured more coffee.

He noticed an antique poster on the wall of the suite for the Hanoi Exposition in January 1903, a relic of French colonial rule. It showed Marianne, the French goddess of liberty, leaning on her sword and at her feet, a beautiful Vietnamese woman sitting on the ground, holding up a fan. Below it, sitting on a table, he spotted the book My Hanh's father, Thành, had left for him in Hanoi. He'd brought it to read on the trip. He grabbed it and pulled off the string still wrapped around the leather cover. It was an English-language biography of the great Vietnamese General Vo Nguyen Giap. Robert lay it before him and opened it. There, as the morning light poured through the window, he read Thành's inscription, written in the shaky penmanship of a dying man. *Dear Robert – may spring come to the snow-covered volcano. Thành*

The snow cold, hard, icy; a volcano hot, volatile, ready to explode; spring, a rebirth, a safe place between the extremes. A safe place? Hardly. Maybe Allen is right. I shouldn't go. Play safe. Keep my distance. Then he remembered what My Hanh had said at Ngoc Son Temple on Jade Island. *"Making peace means letting go of the past. Returning the sword."* He exhaled a sigh, looked at the clock on the mantel, and realized it was time to leave to meet her at the embassy.

Chapter 9

Robert put on his jacket, walked briskly down the corridor, briefcase in hand, Thành's gift tucked under his right arm, and stopped in front of the elevator doors. He'd decided to bring the book to discuss the inscription with My Hanh after the meeting. *We share a child! Is there still a chance for us? Us? Is that possible?* He glanced at himself in the gilded mirror next to the elevator, straightened up, pressed the button, and took a second, longer look. *Shit, I've got bags under my eyes! I look like fucking Irwin!* Others surrounded him, waiting for the elevator, but he stood, motionless, his thoughts in a dark cloud he knew well, the harbinger of storms to come, self-doubts obscuring the light. *Should I have gotten involved? The kid has a father. He doesn't need me...or maybe My Hanh is right...maybe he does. Either way, we can't lose him. I can't lose him. Not again. Not if I can help it.*

The elevator doors opened, and hotel guests spilled out. Robert entered and saw that the small, round light next to the "L" button was already lit. He smiled at the elderly woman standing before him who'd pressed it. *Why is she dressed in black? An omen?* He chuckled and cast away the negative thoughts. The elevator made a loud humming noise as the carriage descended and bounced mightily when it stopped.

Robert emerged into the lobby and decided to stop at the hotel shop to buy breath mints. Altoids were a steady part of his diet to cover the smell of alcohol that was often on his breath. They'd become an odd comfort food even when he had not taken a drink. He scanned the shelves in the store, looking for anything else he might need to have sent up to the room. After paying for the mints, he walked out of the shop and re-entered the lobby. A bearded man wearing a keffiyeh—the man from the bar the day before—appeared in the corridor connecting the lobby to the hotel's side entrance on Avenue Gabriel. A second bearded man wearing a keffiyeh entered the lobby from the corridor beside the elevator. The two men walked toward Robert as he neared the hotel exit and hurriedly joined him, one on each side.

He swung his head around. "What's this?"

The man on the left pulled a pistol with a silencer from his robe and placed it against Robert's side.

"What the—" Robert said horrified.

"Stay calm, Mr. Samberg," the man said in a heavy Middle Eastern accent hiding the gun in the folds of the robe. "Follow along and you won't get hurt."

He could feel the steel of the pistol barrel. They exited the hotel and walked to a waiting black sedan with darkened windows.

"Get in the back," the man with the gun instructed.

As soon as Robert got in, a third man, already in the back seat, threw a hood over his head, and the car sped away.

Chapter 10

"I don't understand," My Hanh said nervously. "His hotel is just across the street." She looked at Bertrand. "I'm certain he was coming."

"Some friend," he whispered. "We've waited a half hour. He's not coming."

My Hanh and Bertrand stood in the hallway, outside the "tank," a secure communications center at the American Embassy. Ambassador Tom Curley, Chief of French Intelligence, Pierre Leroux, and CIA Chief of Station, Bill Brooks stood a few feet away conferring. Curley opened the door to a conference room and motioned for everyone to enter.

"Any word on Samberg?" he asked, looking at Leroux.

"He ordered breakfast from room service this morning, visited the hotel shop," Leroux reported. "Maybe he changed his mind."

"No, he was coming. Something's wrong," My Hanh said.

"What about An?" Curley asked, again directing the question to Leroux.

Leroux leafed through a thick sheaf of notes in a police file. "There's nothing new on An. We've been looking. . . he attends classes at the École Polytechnique at the Sorbonne, pays the rent for his apartment on time, goes to the movies on the Champs-Élysées. He took out five books on Mao from the library."

"Mao is his hero," Bertrand said, glancing at his watch and shifting in his chair.

Leroux pulled a photo from the file. He held it up and showed it to the others. It was An standing with a bearded, dark-skinned man in front of the Grand Mosque of Paris.

"What's he doing at a Mosque?" My Hanh asked, looking at Leroux and Bertrand.

The photo slipped from Leroux's hand and fell face down on the conference room table. He reached to pick it up and noticed the initials, RY, written in small letters on the back.

"Let me see that," Bertrand said. He took the photo from Leroux and examined it closely. "It's Ramzi Yousef," he said, startled.

"Who?" My Hanh asked, motioning for the photo.

"He's Kuwaiti." Bertrand spoke cautiously. "We know him. He's connected with a radical Islamic group. We have them under surveillance in Kuwait. We thought he was in London, studying English and engineering. We didn't know he'd come to Paris."

"Where did the police get the picture?" Brooks asked.

"A professor at the École Polytechnique found it on the floor of his classroom and gave it to the gendarme who interviewed him about An," Leroux said.

"What class?" My Hanh asked.

Leafing through the report, Leroux responded, "Chemistry."

"An doesn't take Chemistry," Bertrand said.

"The professor said An's name was on the class list. He also gave the gendarme a note from An, requesting research materials for a paper," Leroux said. "Here it is, Research Paper by An Delaunay—the properties of liquid nitroglycerin."

"Isn't that—" My Hanh asked.

"Yes," Brooks responded, his voice dropping an octave, "it's the chemical used for making high-powered explosives, the kind used to bring down buildings."

Brooks looked at Curley. "This is a whole new ballgame."

"Send a cable to Hoffers. We need to run this upstairs," Curley instructed.

My Hanh stood up and looked at the others. "What are you going to do to find them?"

"When I hear from Hoffers, I'll call you," Curley said. "For now, this meeting is over."

Chapter 11

" I can't see, goddamn it!" As a boy Robert was afraid of the dark. He fought with his mother to keep the light on in his room at night. Anything was possible if he could only see. Nothing was possible in the dark. The rough texture of the burlap hood itched and chaffed his skin and made breathing difficult. He could hear the traffic, the whine of motorcycles, the blare of car horns, and sirens in the distance. *Where are they taking me? Count the minutes. Does anything sound familiar?* The darkness amplified the sounds and his fear. His captors occasionally spoke in a language he did not recognize. He'd become woozy from breathing the carbon dioxide trapped inside the hood. "I can't breathe either!" Any attempt to reach up and loosen it brought the hard thrust of a gun barrel back into his side. It was as if he had been plucked from the streets by the CRS in 1968 or abducted by aliens—trapped in an episode of *The Twilight Zone*, his favorite old TV show. Suddenly, after what seemed like an eternity, the car stopped.

"Get out, Mr. Samberg." He felt the gun at his back and a hand gripping his right arm, tugging him forward. He followed along. They stopped a short distance from the car, and he heard the sound of numbers pressed on a keypad and the familiar buzz and clank when a door lock was opened remotely. Standing still, his mind raced. *Twenty-eight minutes from start to stop...where are we?* He felt the cold, noticed gusts of wind ruffling his clothes. For a moment, he smelled the unmistakable aroma of freshly baked baguettes before the wind carried it away. He tried to remember everything in minute detail as he'd seen in all the crime shows over the years on sleepless nights. Even the smells. Maybe this would save his life like it did on TV.

He heard the lock disengage and the creaking sound of the hinges as the door opened. They walked through an area with uneven cobblestones, then up five flights of stairs that Robert dutifully counted—*48, 49, 50. Fifty steps.* They stopped abruptly at the top of the stairs. Another door opened and they rushed inside. One of the kidnappers dragged him across the room and shoved him down onto the hard surface of a small wooden chair. Still unable to see, he fell onto the chair awkwardly and almost tumbled off. There was a moment of silence. The fear rose within him.

Suddenly, and without warning, a kidnapper yanked the hood from his head. The rough texture of the burlap scraped his skin. It burned. Robert winced and squinted from the bright sunlight that flooded the room through a bank of tall French windows along the wall. There before him, wearing jeans and a black sweatshirt, perfect garb for a cold autumn day at the Sorbonne, an opaque look on his face, the burlap hood dangling in his right hand, stood An.

"What the fuck? What are you doing?" Robert said slack-jawed in a voice that was at once enraged and dismayed.

"Do as I say, Robert," An said forcefully. He handed him a slip of paper with a bank account number and his name, An Delaunay, scrawled on it, along with a heavy, brick-shaped mobile telephone. The three kidnappers, their faces hidden by keffiyehs, stood on the opposite side of the room with machine guns strapped over their shoulders and pistols at their sides.

"Call your bank in New York. Tell them to wire $100,000 to the account. Once the transfer is made, you will be released."

Robert looked down at the paper, then over at the three kidnappers. He reeled from the shock of the moment but steeled himself. He glanced at his watch and raised his voice so the others could hear. *Keep your head. Keep your head.* "This won't work. It's too much money to wire overseas. It will have to be broken up, and that will require the approval of a bank officer. They'll ask questions. They'll report it to banking authorities who can trace it back to you." He spoke calmly as if issuing instructions to an office secretary.

An did not respond. He turned and gestured to one of the kidnappers, who walked over and placed the barrel of his machine gun at Robert's head. He spoke slowly, ominously. "You own America's largest radio network; your office is on the top floor of the World Trade Center; and you tell us you can't get your bank to wire money!"

Robert felt the adrenalin pump throughout his body. He stiffened like a cat with its back stretched in an arc, its hair raised, its legs ready to spring forward. He labored to control his breathing and keep his balance. He looked at his watch. "It's 4:15 in the morning in New York. The banks are closed. I can't do this now," he said as he looked at An, pleading. *Make them believe me!*

"You are a Jew, a swine, an enemy of Islam!" The kidnapper thrust the machine gun barrel forward, knocking Robert's head to the side and gashing his skin.

Panic-stricken, he gritted his teeth and hissed, "An, what the fuck?"

An raised his voice, chanting unblinkingly like a student rebel at a protest march. "Do it, Robert, just do it."

Robert kept his composure. He thought back to his student days when he led the *enragés* against the CRS in the Latin Quarter, the strength he felt then, the strange calm that came over him as he assumed leadership in the midst of a war zone on rue Saint-Jacques. He looked the kidnapper in the eyes, the only part of his face visible through the black-and-white-checkered keffiyeh. They were black too, like the eyes of a shark. "I'm telling you," Robert said firmly, "I can't get you the money this way. It won't work. Give me some time, give me the night and I'll come up with a plan that will work. I want to live. I'll get you the money. Do you understand?" He looked to An again. "Tell them I'll do it."

An approached the kidnapper, who lowered his gun and motioned for An to follow him to the other side of the room. Robert watched as the two of them huddled, speaking softly in English and French. He discerned an occasional word but couldn't hear well enough to understand what they were saying. They returned to Robert.

The kidnapper pointed the machine gun at his head again and

spoke firmly. "You have until midnight tomorrow Paris time, 6:00 pm New York time, to get the money. We want it in dollars in a suitcase left behind the bushes on the west side of the statue of Louis XIII in the park below. If you fail, you're dead." He motioned for An to step forward and gave him a set of handcuffs and a key. "Take him in the bedroom and cuff him to the bedpost." He waved the machine gun as An and Robert moved forward and locked the bedroom door behind them—father and son together, in a terrifying family reunion.

Chapter 12

Robert turned and looked at An. "You fucking told them about me!" He seethed, pushing his son and knocking them both off balance. Blood dripped from Robert's temple onto the parquet floor. He raised his arm and pressed the sleeve of his designer dress shirt against the laceration.

"Just get them the money," An responded, regaining his balance, his tone stalwart. "Move over to the bedpost."

"What the fuck do you think you're doing?" Robert said, his eyes wide open, glaring as his son attached the cuffs, first to his wrist, then to the mahogany post of the double bed.

"What I think needs to be done," An replied, looking at Robert's wound, which had by now stained a large area of his shirt sleeve.

"What *you* think? You're a college kid!" Robert shouted, yanking his arm and rocking the bed. Robert shook his head. "My Hanh called me in Florida, asked me to help mobilize a search for you." He glanced at his watch. "Right now, she's at the American Embassy with Bertrand at the meeting I set up. I was on my way to join them when your Arab friends grabbed me."

"I know all that, and I really don't care."

"You don't care that your stepmother and your father are worried sick about you? You don't care about your family?" Robert asked, flabbergasted. "How can you be even a tiny bit Vietnamese and not care about your family?"

"I worship at the altar of my ideology, not my family! Just get the money," An said, his voice cold.

Robert looked ahead, trying to think of a way to reach him, to find out what had driven him to join with Middle East radicals. If he could figure that out, maybe he would find a way to draw him away. "Tell me about the others, their movement? Who are they?"

An did not respond right away. He turned and looked again at the bloodstain on Robert's shirt sleeve. "They're my friends from school. They believe in their cause as I do in mine." An reached back and pulled the hood of his sweatshirt over his head. It was chilly in the room.

"What *is* your cause?" Robert asked.

"The opposite of yours," An responded.

"Explain." Robert shifted back and forth on his feet to keep warm.

An smirked. "Let me guess. You celebrated when the Berlin Wall fell, right? I opposed it. You approved when Solidarity won in Poland. I hated it. You denounced the Chinese Communist Party crackdown on the pro-democracy protests in Tiananmen Square. I loved it."

"Yes, opposite," Robert said, shaking his head. "I'm happy the West is winning the cold war. I see you are not."

"We're also on different sides in the Middle East. Ramzi invited me to meetings of the Islamic movement at school, rare for a non-Muslim," An explained.

"Ramzi? Is he the one who ripped my skin with the barrel of the machine gun?"

"Yes, we call him RY, from Kuwait," An said. "He wants to make Islam great again."

"Like in the 13th century?" Robert asked incredulously.

"Yes...he'll let you go if you get the money."

"Christ, An! You don't know that!"

"To them, America is the enemy of the Islamic revolution. To me, it's the enemy of the socialist revolution."

"So, you kidnap your stepmother's friend and blackmail me to finance their cause?"

An began to shift back and forth too. "When you have a higher purpose—"

"Kidnapping, blackmailing...are okay." *I see.*

"Yes," An replied, his voice sounding less certain.

"Risking your family, losing them...that's okay too?"

"Yes. Yes."

"I once risked losing my father, when I helped Thành in Paris. He didn't understand my politics," Robert said.

"Like you don't understand mine," An said.

"I made a choice that still haunts me," Robert said, wistfully.

"An American hero!" An mocked.

Robert responded, shaking his head, "You really don't deserve my saving your ass."

"It's not my ass on the line," An said. "It's yours."

"Right." *I need to make this about him, about us.* "Look...I want to help you, even though we appear to live on different planets."

An looked at him coldly. "I don't need your help," he said. "You need mine, and the only way I can help you—"

"I know...is if I get the money."

"Right." An looked at him. "You've got plenty of it."

"You don't understand," Robert said.

"Neither do you."

"Help me, then."

"You're beyond help, with so much blood on your hands—napalm, Agent Orange in Vietnam—your thirst for oil in the Middle East."

"You think RY and his crew are any better?"

"You just don't get it, Robert."

He closed his eyes. *Nothing I say is helping me reach this kid...and he's right, America has often done wrong. It's like the arguments about the war I used to have with my father. Two people who saw the same facts and drew opposite conclusions. Gaps in thinking too wide to bridge.*

A gust of wind blew up against the window in the bedroom and made a cracking sound. Robert snapped out of his daze. He looked at his watch, wary of RY's deadline. *Midnight tomorrow. I need to act!* He turned back to his son. "I know you don't trust me, and I'm sure you won't agree, but my gut tells me that if I don't get the ransom, these people, your friends—they'll kill both of us!"

An cast a sharp look at him and took the key from his pocket. He held it up for a moment, walked over, and unlocked the cuffs. "Sit down over there," he said. "You look wobbly."

The blood dripped from his wound. Robert noticed his face in the mirror above the dresser as he moved toward the chair—as white as snowflakes on a winter day.

"Are you getting the money?" An asked, his voice softening ever so slightly.

Robert sat up. "I'll need the cell phone."

An looked at Robert and saw a determined expression cross his face.

For a moment, they fell silent, bound by a bloodline that one knew about and the other did not. Robert gazed at the room before him, extravagantly large, with curved walls, French windows, gilded furniture, and gold leaf, a Baroque style for a medieval moment. In the fireplace across the room, embers burned from a fire that had recently gone out. Robert smelled the smoke. He listened to the breathing of his son standing nearby.

Years before, he'd stood next to his own father in a trout stream in Montana, their lines hopelessly tangled. He heard the water swirling around them and his father's words.

"I found a radio station for sale and I'm going to New York next week to buy it. I want you to quit your job and join me. I need you. I want your name on the sign next to mine. And when I retire it will all be yours. Father and son together—unstoppable, unshakable. There's nothing we can't do together, Robbie...I need you!"

"Put the cuffs back on me and call RY," he instructed An as he moved back to the bedpost.

An did as he was told and yelled, "RY, phone!"

They heard footsteps outside the door, the noise of a key inserted into the lock. The bedroom door opened. RY entered, looked at An, then handed Robert the phone. "No tricks!"

"I can't use it cuffed to the bed," Robert said, quickly adding, "No tricks."

RY nodded to An to remove the cuffs. Robert pulled out his card with phone numbers from his wallet and fumbled with the boxy device, trying to figure out how to dial long distance. He reached Allen Hoffer's home phone in Washington. There was no answer. Next, My Hanh's in Paris. Robert let the phone ring again and again, taking time to figure out his next move. RY stood a few feet away, aiming his machine gun at Robert. An sat down on the chair. Suddenly, the battery light on the phone came on.

"Stop the stalling, RY said, "or you'll die." He thrust the gun toward Robert.

"I'm not stalling," he said as he dialed Andi in New York, then in Florida. The battery light on the phone began to blink.

"Do you have a charger?" Robert asked. RY responded with an angry stare.

"Shit!" Desperate, he dialed the person he least wanted to ask for help.

"Thank God I got you," he said when Irwin picked up.

"Do you know what time it is? You woke me out of a dead sleep. Again!"

"I need you to get a $100,000 cash, hide it at the bottom of a suitcase, and bring it to Paris on the Concorde."

"Um…what is this?"

"I need it here tomorrow. Tell no one. I don't have time to explain. I need your help, Dad, and I need it right now," Robert pleaded desperately. There was silence on the other end of the line. The battery light blinked faster.

"I should know better," Irwin said.

"Dad, please, it's urgent—it's not—"

"Another millionaire's trinket?"

"No, Dad, it's not, it's—"

"Okay. Okay. I'll get it done, where do we bring it?" Irwin said, tight-lipped.

Oh, shit…the statue…Louis XIV or Louis XIII? The name of the park? Fuck! The phone is about to die. "Go see my friend, Pierre Le Rest, bartender at the Hotel Crillon—he'll give you instructions. And remember, not a word to anyone else." Robert spoke quickly as the battery light blinked faster still.

"Alright, Robert. But it won't be me—my passport has expired. The only one I can trust with this is Dick Dellmore. I'll send Dick." With that, the battery ran out; the phone died.

"Fuck!" Robert cried under his breath.

Chapter 13

After the meeting at the embassy, My Hanh walked to the Tuileries Gardens, following the path she and Robert had taken so many times twenty-two years before, through the ornate wrought-iron gates, onto the gravel walkway that cut through the center of the gardens, past the grand circular fountain.

She arrived at the large oak tree with the hole at the base of its trunk, a place where her memories with Robert lingered and her imagination soared. It was their special corner of the garden next to a stone wall with dense shrubs all around where in '68 she had left him secret messages from her father to jumpstart peace talks, and where on a warm summer night long ago, they'd made love. A cold autumn wind rustled the red, orange, and yellow leaves on the ground and in the surrounding forest. She stood silently, stared at the tree, and imagined Robert sitting on the ground, his back to the great oak, reading the letter she had left for him. She saw a tear in his eye as he learned that she had returned to Hanoi and would terminate her pregnancy.

Her life since then had not gone as planned. Living a lie about their son, marrying Bertrand as a cover to protect her career, disappointing her father with her political ambition, smashing the norms of her culture and her upbringing. As a teenager, she had gone on a hunger strike to support her right to study in Paris. She had challenged the Confucian role for women that had become part of Vietnam's culture. She had refused an arranged marriage set up by her family. She had allowed herself a love affair with an American in Paris in the middle of the American War.

My Hanh stood alone in the garden as the sun fell in the sky. In her mind's eye, she spoke to Robert as she had in Hanoi, telling him again about the history of Vietnam's heroines, the role they played in defense of the nation. She wanted him to understand why she left—why she put her ambition for the women of her country, for the party, and the nation above all else. She had tried to explain this on Jade Island, and just the day before at the bar at the Crillon, but she was unsure that he truly understood.

She looked up at the clouds and saw the figures of the Trung sisters leading the battle for independence against the Han Chinese. She saw herself standing at the side of Trieu Thi Trinh as she fought against the oppression of the Wu Chinese. She saw herself riding with King Quang Trung's Commander-in-Chief, the brave woman, Bui Thi Xuan, leading elephant-mounted warriors against a quarter million Qing Chinese invaders in 1789, the year of the French Revolution. My Hanh stood with another woman, Marianne, the French goddess and the personification of liberty, equality, fraternity, and reason. She adored Joan of Arc, the "Maid of Orléans," heroine of France in the Hundred Years' War. These women, like the heroines of Vietnam, were her inspiration. They lived in her heart along with the lingering question, "Can I live up?"

As the sun fell behind dark clouds and the winds picked up, My Hanh stood before the oak tree, still seeing Robert's face, searching for what was in his heart, and beginning to realize what was in hers. She feared for him and their son, believing that they were in danger and that the help they needed would not be forthcoming. If no one else would save them, she would. With the colorful leaves blowing up around her, she turned and left the great oak, marched through the garden at a determined pace, and found her way to the metro at the corner of Place de la Concorde and Rue de Rivoli. She took the train to the office of Vietnam's Embassy in Paris near the Bois de Boulogne.

"Robert is missing, too," My Hanh told Allen Hoffers, after waiting ten minutes on a transatlantic call for him to come to the phone.

"I know. I just got off the phone with Curley and Brooks. They filled me in. Sorry to keep you waiting," Allen said in a businesslike manner.

"Allen, there's something wrong here."

"Well, it could also be something innocent—you know Robert..."

The slight did not get by My Hanh. "I think you should give your friend the benefit of the doubt."

"I didn't mean it like—"

"It sounded like you did," she said, pressing him.

"Look, they'll find them. The French police are good at this. They're cooperating with the embassy."

"Are you tracking Ramzi Yousef?" My Hanh asked bluntly.

No response. "I can't speak about that."

"Allen, I need you to level with me."

"Look, I know about you...your capabilities, but we don't have diplomatic relations. I took your call because of Robert. I offered my help because of him, but getting into classified matters—I just can't go there."

"My instincts are screaming that there's something dangerous here," My Hanh warned. "The explosives...you're underestimating the danger of Islamic fundamentalism."

"It's 1990. We're the most powerful nation on Earth. Whatever the danger, I think we can handle it."

"I don't think you're as ready as you think you are."

"I'm not going to get into our intelligence on Yousef, or anyone else. Curley and Brooks are on it. They'll find them."

"That's not good enough! I spoke to Curley and Brooks at the embassy. They are babysitting gendarmes doing a 'by the book' missing persons investigation. This is my son, Robert's son!"

"I know."

My Hanh spoke forcefully. "I want a full covert op, all assets in play. That's what it will take. Do you hear me?"

"I think you're letting your emotions cloud your judgment."

My Hanh raised her voice. "Allen, with my family, emotions *are* my judgment! There are two lives at stake here—the most important lives!"

Allen refused to budge. "I'll have to run your request up the chain of command. I'll get back to you."

"Don't forget I can make or break the new initiative between our two countries." My Hanh slammed down the phone. She closed her eyes and paused to catch her breath.

The phone rang. It was Bertrand. "I have bad news. We just received an Arabic intercept from Kuwait, a message to Yousef—it says the infidels in Paris must die."

"Will the French act on this?" she asked impatiently.

"I have tried, but I can't get the bureaucracy to move."

"What about your comrades in the French party?"

"They're powerless, useless," he said.

"Your colleagues at the Ministry of Foreign Affairs?"

"They see this as a police matter."

"What about the gendarmerie?" she asked.

"I reached out. I pushed. They see it as a missing persons issue. The Americans, the French, these people have no idea what they are dealing with," Bertrand said, adding, "They don't understand the danger."

"I need you to get me a list of the locations where Yousef has stayed in Paris. Can you get it?" My Hanh asked.

"I don't know. It might take some time."

"I'll need surveys of city center, aerials of rooftops and climbing gear. Can you get that?"

"I'm not sure—"

"Bertrand, damn it! I need you to get these!"

"But you don't have their location."

"I need that too! You need to get it for me," she commanded.

"You'll need authorization from Chairman Vo."

"I know. He's my next call."

"Alright then. I'll do what I can," he said.

"Damn it, Bertrand, I need—"

"Okay, okay."

After a pregnant silence, "Merci, Bertrand." My Hanh hung up.

The phone rang again.

"You didn't hear this from me, but Yousef is the leader of a cell planning an attack in the United States."

"What are you going to do about it, Allen?" My Hanh asked.

"We won't move until we find out where the attack will take place. In the meantime, all I can tell you is that we are ramping up surveillance."

"You're risking the life of a prominent American and my son."

"I know that. But my hands are tied."

"Mine are not."

"I need you to share the intel, all of it."

"My H—"

"Allen, I've got my father's papers from '68, and your name is all over them! Remember your trip to Paris?"

"What?"

"Robert told me about Dellmore and the challenge. Whatever evidence he has, I have ten times more, and you are part of it," My Hanh warned.

"You can't—"

"Allen, I want action, and if I don't get it, you will be labeled a bigger communist sympathizer than Robert—much bigger." My Hanh cast her words boldly.

"Who the hell do you think you're threatening!"

"If he goes down, you go down!"

"Unless I what?"

"Full intel support for a covert op, now!" she snapped.

There was a long, difficult pause. "Damn you, My Hanh! Okay, okay...if you're putting it all on the line," Allen said, "but it's just between us—nobody else. I'm going off the playbook, and we need to go off the grid."

"I need to know where they are."

"We don't have that yet."

"As soon as you do, I need you to pass it to me."

"How can I reach you, off the grid?"

"The tree—in the Tuileries Garden," she said.

"History repeats itself. Yes, I'll have Brooks leave it in the hole at the base of the oak tree."

"There's not much time."

"Code for a pickup?" Allen asked.

"How about Hoan Kiem."

"The Lake in Hanoi where you met Robert?"

"Yes, perfect!" My Hanh said.

"Alright, when you get the code, check the tree. But no guarantees. Goodbye, My Hanh." Allen hung up.

She took a breath, then dialed Chairman Vo Chi Cung in Hanoi. It took a few minutes for the call to get through six thousand miles away.

"Mr. Chairman, greetings to you from Paris. We've got a situation here."

"I know. I have been briefed by the ambassador," he said. "We are very troubled about your stepson and the American. I just met him at your father's funeral, and I read your report about the work you did with him at the Ngoc Son Temple."

"Mr. Chairman, our special group...I would like to bring them here. We can handle this."

Cung spoke emphatically. "A terrorist from the Middle East in Paris is not our concern, My Hanh. We are pushing the French—"

"But they're holding my stepson!"

"An has a French father. He is kidnapped in France. It's a French problem."

"Chairman Vo, I insist—

"Work with the French and let them handle it."

"I met with their intelligence chief, Leroux, and they're dragging their feet. An's life is at stake."

"The Politburo has decided. You must stand down. It's your duty."

"If my father were alive..." My Hanh mused, way out of line.

"My Hanh, there is much sympathy over the death of your father, but if he were alive, he would instruct you as I have. Now stand down, especially if you want to protect your career."

"Chairman Vo!" she implored, then fell silent. "Thank you, Mr. Chairman," she added, tight-lipped, knowing she had overstepped, then hung up the phone. She stood up, shook with rage, closed her eyes, and with a loud grunt, smashed her right elbow into the solid wood table in front of her, breaking it in two.

She opened her eyes and saw an image of her mother, the woman who had always stood by her side. She picked up the phone and dialed her number at their ancestral home in the Bac Son Valley, Vietnam.

"Your voice. What's wrong, my daughter?"

"It's your grandson—and that man!"

"Robert?"

"Yes, Robert!"

"What about An?"

"He's missing—in trouble, big trouble. The situation is impossible."

"You must do whatever it takes to help him, even the *im*possible!"

"Mother, I've been ordered to stand down. I'm out there by myself on this."

"You have at your command all the strength you require. Take mine, too, and the strength of our heroines who have done the impossible before."

"Mother, you and your comrades did the impossible. You defeated two Western powers, France and America, but the world has changed. It's more complicated."

"I have faith in you, my daughter." My Hanh smiled.

"What about the American?" her mother asked.

"We think he's with An."

"Father and son together?"

"Yes, but he doesn't know it. He doesn't know about Robert."

"You still haven't told him?"

"I don't want him to know, Mother. Robert drinks too much, brags too much, collects material things—things that don't matter. He is hard!"

"Yes, and he showed up in your life and is the father of your son," her mother said.

"Mother, I don't need a man to show up for me, especially that man. I am my own keeper."

"My Hanh, you are strong, you can stand in any storm, but you don't always have to stand alone."

"Chairman Vo has ordered me to stand down."

"Another man in your way, my daughter?"

"Yes, another man like in my dream with his foot on my neck."

"My Hanh, listen to your heart. You know what you must do."

"But if I do this, my political career will be over."

"Yes, and something new will start."

"And Robert?" My Hanh asked in a whisper.

"My daughter, sometimes life brings us people who are strangers to themselves, and we must give them time to find their worthiness, especially if they are seeking it. It's a price we pay for love."

"Mother, are you saying—"

"I'm saying that a tough skin often protects a softness inside. Search within your heart, My Hanh."

"Yes."

"Now, I must go, the soup is boiling over."

Chapter 14

The night fell and the temperature dropped, a record cold, the winds whipping across Place des Vosges, the great square five floors below. Robert stood handcuffed to the bedpost. An sat at the edge of the bed. The shadows of sunset moved across the gilded wall coverings. A fresh log burned in the fireplace, offering scant warmth and casting a flickering light on the two figures. Robert's gash had congealed, and a scab had begun to form. The blood on his shirt had dried to a dark red stain. Two empty bowls with dried remnants of rice and vegetables sat on the table across from the fireplace. It was their only meal, tasteless and taken without enjoyment. Robert thought of things he wanted to say to An, questions he wanted to ask, but couldn't muster the right words.

"I'm trying to put myself in your shoes," he finally said.

"Why bother?"

"Well, it's something I can't explain," Robert said softly.

"I thought you Americans have an answer for everything!"

"Yeah—we're proud of our 'can-do' spirit, but it's not the whole story."

"What is the whole story?"

Robert hesitated. He reached up and touched the wound on his temple. "One part aspiration, two parts self-delusion..."

"Oh my god, do I hear self-criticism?" An said, mockingly.

Robert clenched his fist, pursed his lips, and looked away. "You might if you drop the fucking attitude."

An sneered. "Asshole," he said under his breath.

"I get called that all the time. You're not the first," Robert said, self-reflectively, shifting tone.

"Why is that?" An said, condescension etched on his face.

"Because when I want something, I push hard, and if someone gets in the way..." Robert took his free hand, extended his index finger, and sliced it across his neck.

"Heads roll! Very French!" An said, chuckling.

"I push hard because my father pushed hard. He pushed hard because he had five brothers and he had to push hard to matter."

"Like father, like son?"

Robert stared at him. Every fiber of his being wanted to tell him the truth. "I remember when my father hired me. I asked him what the most important thing was he expected from me. He didn't hesitate. 'Obedience,' he said. Then he told me about his idol, the American movie mogul Louis B. Mayer. He said that when Mayer gave an order at MGM Studios, everyone obeyed, and if they didn't..." Robert ran his index finger across his neck again.

"A typical American," An said disapprovingly. "Cowboys conquering the Wild West, rugged individualism."

"Yes—we idealize strong men. We strike the mighty pose, conjure how things ought to be, but that's a cartoon version of how things really are."

"Like General Westmoreland's body counts—made it look like you were winning the war while you were actually losing," An said.

"Sometimes, America screws up, like we did in Vietnam. We buy into an idea that trips us up—like anticommunism did after the Second World War, after China fell."

"When Mao took power!" An perked up.

"Yes, when China went communist, Americans became afraid, and we allowed a demagogue to play upon our fears—Senator Joseph McCarthy. McCarthyism."

"You abandoned anticolonialism, betrayed our independence, and supported the return of French rule in our country. That's fucking America for you!"

"Not our finest moment."

"So, you admit it. Your America is a lie! Mao said idealism is easy, because people can talk as much nonsense as they like without having it tested against reality. Your reality is different than your promise."

"Our constitution says, 'We the people, in order to form a more perfect union...' Well, guess what, we're still not perfect. We fall short of our ideals. But at least in America, when we screw up, there's usually somebody who stands up and tries to fix things."

"You're delusional, Robert!" An scoffed.

"Look, An, one of us, maybe both, will probably die here, and I don't feel much like a political debate."

"That's because you have no defense for America. There is none!"

"Free people are imperfect people. We fuck up. We fall short. But our ideals are noble, and that has to count for something," Robert said. "It's like we're piloting this airplane from New York to Paris. The winds are always blowing us off course. But we believe in the destination, so we take the controls and steer the plane back on course, and one day we'll arrive there. Our destination is democracy, human rights, free speech, free press, opportunity and equality, the idea that Americans can move up the social and economic ladder through hard work and perseverance."

"That's your explanation for what America did in Vietnam? Flying the plane off course?"

"It's complicated. There were so many forces at play, some good, some bad—yes, we got way off course. We lost 58,000 of our own. We did ourselves and your country great harm, but then, painfully, we self-corrected. Our political system worked. We withdrew, and Nixon was forced to resign."

"In Vietnam, our culture says that a person or a society with good fortune will face a downfall if they live in an unworthy manner. That's America. That's America's fate. You can't escape it by saying it was just a moment off course on a worthy journey."

"Can't the opposite be true as well?" Robert asked. "Can't the unworthy change their fate through good deeds?"

"Yes, and what about you? What were your deeds?"

"I told you, when I was your age, I opposed the American War. That's why I helped Thành. Opposing the war was my passion—like Mao is yours."

"Careful what you say about Mao."

"Mao killed a lot of innocent people—thousands in the Great Leap Forward, thousands more in the Cultural Revolution."

"The price of revolutionary change," An said defiantly.

"Oh, so it's okay when Mao kills innocent people, and not okay when Americans do it."

"Mao didn't kill for greed."

"Tell that to the mothers who grieved their sons."

"And the sons who grieve their mothers," An said.

"What do you mean?" Robert asked.

"My real mother was killed in your air campaign, Operation Rolling Thunder, just after I was born. And my father—"

"Your father?"

"I never knew him. I was adopted." His face sank. "No more nonsense about your noble ideals. The 'can-do' spirit of your CIA hung Vietnamese like my mother by their feet and thumbs, used waterboarding, electric shocks to genitals, and solitary confinement. My mother rotted in a dark cell, a dark, dank, dirty—very dirty cell," An said defiantly.

Robert could not respond. He looked over at his son, saw his head bowed, and noticed the tears running down his cheek, illuminated by the light of the fire. "I'm sorry, An."

"She was probably raped by one of your soldiers—my real father. She died a hero, carrying supplies, food, and ammunition on her bicycle to a battle. In the South, our women were 40% of the guerilla and militia forces. An American bomb exploded near her, killing her and the woman who walked with her, holding the bamboo pole attached to the handlebar of the overloaded bike to keep it steady."

Such a cruel tale! No wonder he's become a radical!

"It's the reason I joined the party."

Robert looked at his son incredulously.

"Don't look so shocked. There are hundreds of young men and women in Vietnam who have experienced this."

"I tell you, An, Americans did not know about this, about the torture. It was kept from us. A lot was kept from us," he said apologetically.

"That's no excuse.

"At least you have a stepmother who loves you."

"She ignores me. Too busy saving the world to worry about my world. It's the mother I never knew who lives in my heart, not your friend, My Hanh, the politician!"

"Maybe there is a reason." *I cannot tell him the truth.*

"And your stepfather, Bertrand?" Robert asked.

"He's a good communist, but he's a diplomat, always traveling. I'm not a priority for him, either. I've always been on my own," An said forlornly.

"So, you adopted Mao as your father figure?"

"I wish Mao *were* my father. I look up to him. He had guts, vision, the courage of his convictions. He allowed China to stand up after a century of humiliation."

"I disagree. You're forgetting about the death of tens of millions during the Great Leap Forward and the cruelty of the Cultural Revolution. I don't think you're being fair with Bertrand and especially with your stepmother." *Should I?*

"You really don't know her," An said, annoyed.

"Oh, I think I do."

"From a love affair twenty-two years ago?"

"An, sometimes, with a woman, it only takes a glance, a meeting of the eyes, and you know who she is."

"I heard she left you—maybe you missed something?"

"No. No. I should have followed her. I should have broken the rules, come to Vietnam in the midst of war and found her," Robert said dolefully.

"I think you have been watching too many Hollywood movies. Cotton candy versions of love and politics."

"I don't like cotton candy. Gives me a stomachache."

"What about Thành? What was he to you?"

"Thành taught me a lot. He listened to me and asked questions. He got me involved with the peace talks. He liked the reformer, Dubcek, not the radical, Mao." Robert cast a pleading look at An, still hoping to turn him around.

"Thành sold out. He got soft. It's a disease that comes with age," An said, signaling his support for the more radical elements of the party.

"Thành was wise, the kind of wisdom that comes with age. I only wish my father had this, too," Robert said sadly.

"Your father, the strong man, lacked wisdom?"

"If he were wiser, he would have been less selfish. He wooed me away from the life I wanted. He recruited me with talk about standing against the world together, about the pride we would both feel with our names on a sign for a family business. He spoke as if this were the most important thing in the world to him, and I had always wanted to be the most important thing in the world to him." Robert sat up, looked across the darkened room, the fire now having burned down to embers, the temperature again dropping.

"You followed your father's ambition instead of your own?" An asked.

"My life became about showing my father I was worthy of being on that sign with him."

"What was the life you really wanted?" An asked, looking into Robert's eyes for the first time during the conversation.

"Do you want the truth?"

"Yes, the truth."

Robert paused, stared at his son. "I don't know anymore."

"You must be kidding," An said. "A rich, powerful capitalist who doesn't know what he wants? What about the stations you bought?"

"No, it's something more."

"What is it, then?"

"One day, my father invited me to lunch. He looked at me and said there was something he was planning to tell me later but would tell me then. He told me he had heart disease and that his doctor recommended that he retire. He said he had given it much thought and that he was going to appoint his assistant, a new employee, as his successor, instead of me. He said it was for my own good. He had concluded that I could not handle the job of company president. I wasn't up to it. The name on the sign above the door—it would have to be changed. 'Things change' were the words I remember him saying, words seared into my consciousness, the last words he said before he got up and left the restaurant. He didn't even pay the bill."

An looked at Robert. "What did you do?" he asked, bug-eyed.

"I left, started my own company, built it bigger than his—much bigger— and now I stand to buy *his* radio station along with forty-nine others. I didn't realize it until recently, but my life became about making up for the hurt that day he passed me over. I see that now."

"Mao would have approved. Your father stood up against feudalism, the automatic passing of power, wealth and position from father to son."

"To me, it was a betrayal. He made a promise. He broke it. He's my father. A son wants his father to love him, to know him, not to humiliate him." Robert stood facing his own son, the irony of this not lost on him. "Nothing hurts worse than when someone you want to love you doesn't see what you're made of. To this day, I have bad dreams about it. I wake up at night, shaking, sweating, feeling the devastation."

"Why are you telling me this?" An asked, his eyes still on Robert's.

Robert wanted to tell him who he was—who they both were—it hurt badly not to, but he said, "Because—sometimes you live your life thinking a certain way, only to find out that what you once thought made sense suddenly no longer does. Do you understand what I mean?"

"No, I don't think I do," An replied. He spoke with a tenderness and an interest he had not shown before, and he added, looking at Robert's wound, "Does it still hurt?"

"Yes, but it's the least of our problems at the moment."

"Our problems? I think you mean *your* problems."

"No. Someday, I hope you'll understand...look, it's going to be a long night and a long day tomorrow, can we get some sleep?"

"Okay... RY!" Ramzi returned, carrying another log. He looked at Robert, pointing to his watch. Robert had the night and another day to get the money.

Can I trust my father, Dellmore, the men trying to betray me?

Ramzi walked over, threw the log on the fire, and signaled to An to undo Robert's cuffs. "Sleep with one eye open," he told him. "We'll check on you hourly." He left and locked the door.

Robert stretched the arm that had been attached to the bedpost and rubbed his wrist where the cuffs had left a mark. He walked over to the fireplace, turned, and watched as An crawled under the covers and gathered a pillow under his head. He warmed his hands as the log ignited and the fire burned brighter and hotter. After a few moments, he walked over to the bed and climbed in. An had already fallen asleep. Robert closed his eyes.

Pierre doesn't know where we are. I need to reach him before Dellmore arrives with the money.

Robert awakened in a sweat. The room was cold. *The damn dream of my father again.* Suddenly, he realized that An was no longer in the bed next to him. He heard voices from outside the room. He got up and tiptoed to the door, putting his ear to the keyhole. He could hear An and Ramzi talking.

"I *want* to go to New York," An said insistently.

"We want you in there," Ramzi said. "But first, you must prove yourself. You must show us we can trust you."

"What do I need to do?"

"After the drop, the American must die—you must kill him."

Robert gasped for air from the gut punch. He heard footsteps moving away from the bedroom door and the squeaking hinges of the front door as it opened and closed. Then, another set of footsteps coming back toward the bedroom door. The jingle of keys as someone approached on the other side of where he squatted, still listening. He quickly stood up, ran to the bed, and threw the covers over his body. He lay still, eyes closed, and pretended to be asleep, terrified.

Chapter 15

Robert lay on his side facing away from his son and struggled to mimic the peaceful breathing of a body at rest. He heard An wrestle with the covers as he slid back into the bed. He listened carefully but could hear no other sounds coming from the salon in the apartment. *There's no one here but us! My son! Murder me? No!* Suddenly, Robert opened his eyes and rolled over, pinning An to the bed as he grabbed him by the neck.

"What's going to happen in New York?" Robert pushed his face right up against his.

"Let me g—"

"Fuck you! I heard you through the door."

An struggled to free himself, but Robert was larger and heavier and used his weight to keep him pinned, tightening his grip on the young man's neck. Robert's adrenaline soared.

"What are they doing with the money? What am I paying for?"

"I don't know—let go, I can't breathe!" The color had drained from An's face.

"You don't know! You don't know! But you would kill me to get a front-row seat?"

"You don't understand! Let go!"

"Fuck you, you little shit!" Robert said. "I want the truth and I want it now!"

"Let go of my neck!" An began to punch him hard in his side. He reached up and scraped the fresh scab on his temple, drawing blood that ran down Robert's cheek.

He absorbed the blows, ignored the blood, and tightened his grip.

An's lips began to turn blue. "I know what I heard! You're not going to kill me, you fucker!"

"Kill you? You heard wrong!"

Robert felt his son's body writhe beneath him and saw his eyes blink rapidly, then close as he began to black out.

Daddy no, no, no! My father lifted my little body and threw me down on the ironing board. It was the day he put onions on my cheeseburger. I hated onions and he knew it. But he put them on anyway. He said he forgot. How could he forget? I told him every time. "What's wrong with my son," he said. "Not tough enough for a little kick, huh? Not tough enough?" Then he led my sisters Dottie and Lorraine and my best friend, Joey, in a chant. "Eat the onion, eat the onion, eat the onion!" So, I threw the burger at him and ran to my safe space, a nook in the living room next to the front door, once the spot for the house telephone, but later painstakingly transformed into a showcase of glass shelves and mirrored walls by my father. I tucked myself inside and stomped my feet against the wall of mirrors. The glass shelves crashed to the ground all around, my mother's knickknacks shattered, and my father's project was destroyed. He pulled me out in a rage and dragged me upstairs. I lay on the ironing board, uncut by the falling glass and about to be beaten with the brown leather belt my angry father removed from his trousers and held high above me. No! No!

Suddenly, Robert loosened his grip. *I am not my father! I cannot harm him.* An jumped up, ran from the bed to catch his breath, and Robert followed, got in his face, and screamed again. "You're not going to kill me!"

An pushed him away. "Pig!"

"I came here to find you, save you! I'm out a hundred thousand dollars, and you want to thank me by putting a bullet in my head! Asshole!"

"*You're* the asshole! I didn't ask for your help. You're paying to save your*self*, not me!"

Robert lunged at An, raised his hand to slap him, but stopped. "What kind of idiot did My Hanh raise?" He lifted his hand again. "You don't have a clue!"

"You don't know what you're talking about!"

"Kidnapping, extortion, murder, what's your next move?" Robert seethed.

"Revolution!"

"A revolution in New York City? Are you nuts!"

"That day will come. You'll be lucky if you don't live to see it." An ran his index finger across his neck as Robert had done when he spoke about his father.

"What are you going to do, blow up the Statue of Liberty?"

"I don't know, Robert."

"You don't know?"

"I don't, and I wouldn't tell you if I did."

"You know what I think? I think if Ramzi doesn't trust you now he never will—even if you kill me."

"You're in the way, Rob—"

"Maybe that's exactly where I need to be!"

"Just shut up!"

"What are you not telling me?" Robert threw his arms in the air.

"Everything!"

He reached down deep, trying to find the right words. *My life is at stake here, his life, too!* "I know you won't believe this...but I care about you, An."

"Yeah right."

"I want to live...but I also want you to l—"

"Why is that?"

The night he was conceived, we lay beneath the oak tree. "I'm going to show you an old Vietnamese tradition," My Hanh whispered, moving her head next to mine until our noses touched. "Like the Inuit tribe of Alaska," I said, enjoying the feel of her warm nose rubbing the cold tip of mine. "Now we can make love like the Taoists," she whispered. "How?" I asked. "United in the truth of our love...the truth of our love."

Maybe telling him the truth is the only way out for him and for me.

"Why—because I love your mother..."

"My stepmother!"

"I love My Hanh—but, if you're going to kill me, I'm going to tell you the truth. I want you to know who you are."

"What are you talking about?"

"My Hanh is not your stepmother. She's your mother."

"Liar! You'd say anyth—"

"No, An. You were born of love, not hate. You are lost, Son, and you found refuge in hate."

"Son? Did you say, 'Son'?"

"I did...Bertrand loves you like a son...but he is not your father...I'm your father."

"No, that can't be!"

"On my life, which it is—that's the truth," Robert said, a tear rolling slowly down his bloody cheek.

"What are you telling me?" An said, his expression shocked and empty.

"The truth."

An turned and looked away. He walked across the room like a prizefighter staggering before the fall.

"Now I need for you to pretend that you're asleep."

"What? Why?" An said, still reeling.

"Because I must get a message to my friend Pierre. He needs to know where we are so that he can tell Dellmore where to drop the money. Otherwise, we die."

"How are you going to do that?"

"The cell phone is dead." Looking at the French window, he said, "That's how. I'll climb down and find a phone."

"We're five floors up. The slate roof is steep and slick with ice. You'll fall. You'll die."

"If I can hang on to Macallan at a gallop, I can hang on to a roof. I'll find a drainpipe. There must be one."

"Macallan?"

"My horse."

"You're one crazy American."

"Yes."

An leaned against the wall, slid down to his knees, then lay his head in his hands, sobbing.

Robert looked at his watch. "Shit. I've got less than an hour." He ran to the window, turned the handle and swung it open. Before him lay a sheer drop of icy slate and a howling wind. He spotted a drainpipe just off to the left, and ropes—*must be for the window cleaners.* He took a deep breath and climbed outside on the ledge. His breath turned to mist in the cold air. He closed the windows behind him. *This is crazy shit. But there's no other way. I've got to save us.*

Chapter 16

Robert Samberg and An Delaunay stood side by side in the grand salon of the 17th-century apartment overlooking Place des Vosges—American father, Vietnamese son, a family tableau, except for the incessant trembling, the blood dripping on the floor, the handcuffs on the father, the hollowed face of the son, and the fact that one was, or both were, about to die.

Robert kept watch on the row of French windows lining the south side of the gilded room. He looked at the grand square below, now illuminated by spotlights where Dick Dellmore would soon arrive if his message to Pierre had gotten through. He had made it to a payphone on the second floor of a cafe on the corner. It was Pierre's day off, and he got the answering machine. He ran out of time and sprinted back to the drainpipe hidden on the side of the building. He thought about saving himself. *This is about us, not about me. It's about saving my son.*

The ascent was more challenging than the climb down, and he knocked his head on the window frame as he climbed back into the room, reopening the wound on his temple. No sooner than he had dashed back into the bed, one of the terrorists entered the room and led them at gunpoint to the salon.

It was nearly midnight. He turned to An. They hadn't had time to talk since Robert's brief escape. He looked at his son and saw the anguish on his face. In Vietnam, the family was the anchor of life. Sons worshiped at the shrines of their fathers. Robert thought that his revelations must have shattered him. He felt dismay at his son's pained look. *I don't want to die! I don't want him to die!*

He heard the creaking of footsteps on the wooden planks of the ancient floor behind him. A terrorist approached. He turned, smelled the odor of his unclean body and clothing, and caught his lifeless eyes peering from behind a soiled keffiyeh. They were cold, blank, black. The terrorist pointed his Glock 43 pistol at him and, his mouth open, set his feet solidly on the floor. Robert saw in him a fear and a readiness to fire at the first sight of any movement, any gesture, any excuse to kill.

Outside, the winds blew snow against the French windows. Swirls of white powder rose and fell in the geometric gardens below, once the symbol of the king's dominance over nature. Once the place for royal tournaments and spectacles and for duels that left countless noblemen dead on its cold grounds.

As the clock on the roof just above them struck midnight, Robert spotted a husky figure at the center of the square who was trudging through the snow toward the statue of King Louis XIII. He carried a small suitcase that swung back and forth as he walked hurriedly and left deep footprints in the snow.

Robert turned and pointed. "Look there. The man with the suitcase. It's Dellmore! He's making the drop!" He turned his head, first toward the terrorist who stepped toward them, and then to his son. The terrorist handed the Glock to An who stood tall, silent, tightening his grip on the handle of the pistol. Robert watched in horror.

"It's your time, An Delaunay of Vietnam! Time to take vengeance against the American devils!"

Robert stepped back panic-stricken, shuddered with fear, and pointed again to the windows, his arm outstretched, his index finger searching for Dellmore and the suitcase with the money. He fell on one knee and pleaded with his son. "You know who I am. Please, don't do this."

An did not respond. He stood motionless and surveyed the scene before him, the other two terrorists on the far side of the room, each clutching machine guns capable of blasting ten rounds per second. He lifted the Glock, his arm rising up from his side, as a gust of wind rattled the tall windows. The terrorists looked toward Robert and An and lifted their AK-47s, one pointing at An, the other squarely at Robert. There was a momentary silence as the wind died down and life and death hung in the balance. An looked at his father, his eyes opened wide, his face passive.

"An! You know who I am! You can't!" Robert yelled. Another gust blasted the windows, then faded. A two-way radio sitting on a small table suddenly crackled and squawked, then grew silent. It was Ramzi's voice from the square but the wind and the weak signal interfered. The message was unintelligible.

Robert spoke. "What will you say before my shrine? What will you leave there? What will your ancestors say? Do this and you will be lost forever."

An stood silently. The radio erupted with static as Ramzi barked an order from the square. One of the terrorists moved toward the receiver to decipher the message. But again, it was garbled in static.

An glanced around the room at each of the terrorists, his vacant eyes coming to rest on the radio. He coughed and looked at the terrorist closest to him, who had handed him the pistol.

"An!" Robert screamed again.

"Allah 'akbar! Kill him! Kill him now!" Ramzi's voice resounded from the radio throughout the room.

An stood frozen, the Glock pistol aimed at his father. Robert rose to his feet. A gust of cold air burst forth as he, An and the three terrorists suddenly turned toward the French windows, the sound of breaking glass exploding around them. The windows imploded as black-clad figures tore through the glass on ropes suspended outside from the massive slate roof. Robert looked up and saw the blur of silent swinging swords and blood spilling from each of the terrorists, their last cries drowning out the few shots fired and gone awry into the floor or ceiling. He saw the bloody stumps of two heads still rolling from the momentum of the fierce kills.

In the melee, the third terrorist pulled the Glock from An's hand and turned it on him. Without hesitation, Robert charged and seized the gun, protecting An. He struggled with the terrorist, his rage fueling his strength. An stood before them in shock as a commando flew across the room, thrusting a sword through the air with a whisking noise that rivaled the winds outside, now blowing fiercely within the apartment. The blade severed the terrorist's head, but not before a single shot was fired and Robert fell to the floor. The commando rushed to his side, kneeled before him, and threw off a black mask. His body twisted and limp, his consciousness fading, Robert lay in a pool of his own blood. He struggled to open his eyes and glimpsed the blurry figure who cradled his head and looked down at him. "My Hanh!"

Chapter 17

*I*t was bitter cold in the Oval Office at the White House. Snowflakes pelted the large floor-to-ceiling windows behind the Resolute desk, coating the glass with a thick layer of ice crystals. A young Robbie Samberg shivered and gripped a detonator in his left hand, hiding it behind his back. He stood before the 37th President of the United States, Richard M. Nixon, and his National Security Advisor, Henry Kissinger, looked down and wiped the blood away from his horrid wound. The blood pooled on the royal blue carpet. An open bottle of Macallan '26 sat on the table in front of Nixon, a glass half-empty next to it. The room was dark, the only light from a red porcelain lamp on the side table next to the couch. He stood in the devil's den, before him the man who played politics with the issue of war and peace in Vietnam—the man who'd scuttled the Paris peace talks to assure his own election and by doing so, delayed the peace, killing thousands more on both sides, all the while professing to be a man of peace, the son of a Quaker, and a seeker of the greatest title a political leader can attain, "peacemaker."

"Henry, why have you brought this boy here?" Nixon reached over to grab the glass.

"Mr. President," Kissinger said, slowly dragging out his words with a German accent, "he's the boy who met Thành in Paris."

"Communist sympathizer! Traitor! Henry, get him out of here! He's dripping blood on the carpet!"

Young Robbie stood at attention, still hiding the detonator. "Mr. Pres—"

"Don't Mr. President me, son. I read your files! You Jews can't be trusted!"

Young Robbie crossed the room and stood in front of Nixon, blood falling from his chest at the feet of the president. "You should have stopped the war sooner! Thành told me North Vietnam was ready for serious talks in May '68, *but you interfered, monkey wrenched, told South Vietnam to stall—you prom-ised them if they did, you'd offer them a better deal after your election. Do you have any idea how many people died while you protected your election?"*

"Jack Kennedy and his father stole the election of 1960 from me in Chicago! No way I was going to let Lyndon Johnson steal another one in '68 with a last-minute bombing pause and peace conference in Paris. NO WAY!"

Nixon stood up and splashed his right foot in the pool of young Robbie's blood and spoke in the deep, dark voice of the devil. "You say one word about this and I'll make sure—even from my grave—that America will know you're a traitor. You'll lose everything!"

Young Robbie raised his arm and thrust the detonator in Nixon's face. "When I press this, you'll lose everything!"

"Your file said you're a Jew, not a Muslim. Only Muslims blow themselves up, right?" Nixon asked his National Security Advisor.

"Yes, Mr. President." Kissinger spoke calmly, ever the diplomat.

Ramzi Yousef entered the room carrying the suitcase of liquid nitroglyc-erin and wearing his black-and-white-checkered keffiyeh. He raised his fist. "Death to America!" Young Robbie's blood now spread wall to wall.

"What do you want?" Kissinger asked.

"We want our Islamic civilization back! We want Sharia law based on the Koran. But before we build the new, we must destroy the old." Ramzi looked at young Robbie, his finger on the detonator, his blood rising all around them. "Allah 'akbar! Kill them! Kill them! Do it! Do it now!"

"No wait, son," a voice from the corner of the room bellowed in a throaty Southern drawl as a tall man with large ears and furrowed brow waded through the blood and sat down on the couch. It was the 36th President of the United States, Lyndon B. Johnson. "Put it down, son. You don't want to do this. Your contacts with Thành were at my direction. I left a letter to prove it." He looked at young Robbie's wound. "Hmm..." He reached into his brief-case. "Take this and cover the wound. It will stop the bleeding." The president handed him a bandage made from a one hundred thousand-dollar bill.

"No!" Ramzi cried. "Allah 'akbar! Kill them! Kill them! Do it! Do it now!"

Young Robbie groaned and raised the detonator. As he looked down to see his blood now up to his shins, his father Irwin entered the room, wearing his favorite fishing boots to protect him from the rising red tide. He looked at President Johnson. "That boy disappointed me. He let me down. I thought he had it, you know, the killer instinct, the thing you need most to succeed in business, but he just doesn't have it."

"No, father, I do have it. See?" He lifted the detonator. "I have it!"

There was a menacing silence. Irwin looked at Johnson and Nixon, then turned to Ramzi and proclaimed, "He doesn't have it!" He reached out and ripped the one hundred thousand-dollar bill from his son's wound, releasing a fresh torrent of blood.

"Father, how could you? I'm your son. This blood is your blood."

Suddenly, the bulb in the red lamp blinked and went out. The blood had risen above the electric outlet, causing a short.

Young Robbie's son, An, entered the room, holding a lantern, wading through the red sea, a haunted look on his face. He was dressed as a Vietnamese peasant and carried a bag filled with the bones of his ancestors. Young Robbie looked at his son. A single tear fell from his eye. He lowered the detonator.

"Allah 'akbar! Kill them! Kill them! Do it! Do it now!" Ramzi said again.

Looking at An, young Robbie whispered, "His blood is my blood, I cannot—"

Just then, An lunged at his father and wrestled the detonator from his hand. He lifted the red cover protecting the switch used to set off the explosives. Young Robbie's tear became a cascade. He begged his son to put down the detonator, its light flashing red, and watched in horror as An pressed the toggle switch. The room shattered in a thunderclap, and a volcano of fire erupted, boiling blood, scorching souls, rendering the material world hot ash. Swirling snowflakes from the cold night covered what remained in a cloak of icy crystals. As the roof blew away and the walls disintegrated, young Robbie saw a burning book swirling in the air before him—it was the biography of General Giap given to him by Thành. He read the inscription, the thoughts of a dying man who had seen the light in him, Dear Robert - may spring come to the snow-covered volcano. Thành.

Robert opened his eyes and saw the bright lights of the intensive care unit above him. He noticed the blue curtains and the tubes—tubes everywhere. He heard the sounds of the monitors and the pumps propelling fluids into his savaged body. He felt pain where the bullet had passed through his back and exited his stomach. He was groggy, then confused, chilly, nauseated, and most of all, scared—the sensations passed through him like a train racing through a tunnel, each one sucking the scant air left from the one before. He watched the narcotics flow through the tubes into his arm. The room was blurry, a kaleidoscope of light and sound, until, after a few moments, he saw familiar faces and figures standing around his bed—his wife Andi, Allen Hoffers, his father Irwin, and My Hanh.

Unsure if he was still dreaming or awake, a lifetime of grievance rose up uncontrollably, fueled by the lingering effects of the anesthesia and the realization that he had lost all control. Above all, Robert needed to be in control. The fear he felt when he lost it brought out the worst in him. *What happened? What am I doing here? I can't move! Get me the fuck out of here!*

He looked at Andi and blurted, "You don't have it! You don't have it!"

She reached out to touch the top of the thin white sheet covering him. "It's okay, Robert. You're going to be okay. What don't I have?"

He looked at her and scowled. "I'm cold. I'm cold."

She grabbed the spare blanket at the end of the bed and pulled it up over him. "Whatever I don't have, I'll get it for you," she said.

"How can I trust you? You're going to lose it all! You just don't have it!"

A look of dismay crossed her face. She lowered her head and moved away from the bed.

He paused to catch his breath and looked at Allen. "YOU!"

"You're not yourself, buddy," Allen said.

"You, fucking bureaucrat! This is your fault! You and your secret mission! You did this to me!"

Allen backed away and joined Andi, who had left the room to compose herself.

Robert looked up, suddenly overcome by dizziness, then a sharp pain in his neck. He grimaced, and when it passed, he saw his father standing over him. "You're sabotaging my deal, you motherfucker! How could you? I hate you! I hate you!"

"Robert, you've suffered a—"

"You threw away the sign! *Our* sign!" His head rolled left, then right, and he sank back into the pillows propped up behind him. He closed his eyes, reopened them, and saw My Hanh as she placed her hand on Irwin's arm and pulled him away from the bed. He, too, left the room to join the others.

Robert's body shuddered. He began to breathe heavily and couldn't speak. His eyes focused on hers. His tears fell as he remembered. *They killed our son. I tried to save him. I tried! I'm sorry, he's gone! You—* "The turtle...Hoan Kiem," he murmured as he thrust his body forward to reach for her, raising himself as far as the wires and tubes would permit, then let forth a horrid groan and sank back onto the bed.

"Lay down the sword," she whispered, standing over him as she had done in the apartment on Place des Vosges. She touched his hand as he closed his eyes and fell unconscious.

Chapter 18

Robert lay on his back in traction, his head below his feet, positioned so he could see the rolling snow-covered landscape of Auvergne, a remote region in south-central France. This was a land formed eons ago when thunderous volcanic eruptions spewed lava and shaped formations that in the centuries following became the lush farmlands of the rural Massif Central. It was also home to the world-renowned Blaise Pascal Clinic, a hospital for spinal cord injury nestled at the foot of the Chateau du Sailhant, where Robert was taken after his emergency surgery in Paris.

For a man who lived his life in constant motion, this was a regimen of torture with no end in sight. The only respite was that the table was placed next to a wall of French windows. He could look up to the sky and follow the clouds. He could see the open fields in the distance and the rows of dormant volcanos, their peaks covered in white, which dotted the wintry landscape.

"Robert, c'est Pierre. Are you awake?" Pierre asked on the day after the ambulance had brought his old friend to the clinic. It was a bright Sunday afternoon, and he had traveled three and a half hours by train from Paris.

Robert lay with his eyes closed, deep in a melancholy that had befallen him following the shooting. He was still not sure if the sorry scene with Andi, Allen, and Irwin at the hospital had been real or a dream. He could no longer tell the difference. The only thing he remembered with certainty were My Hanh's words, "Lay down the sword," but the memory offered little solace.

"I brought you a treat." Pierre pulled a bottle of *Macallan '26* from a cloth bag, holding it up as Robert opened his eyes. "From your collection." Pierre smiled.

"Nice try," Robert whispered, his voice hoarse. He turned his head aside within his limited range of motion to face toward the windows. "The doctors won't allow it."

"Not for now, for later." Pierre quickly stuffed the bottle back into the bag and placed it on the floor. "I'm sorry to see you this way, Robert—but soon, you'll be back in the saddle!"

Robert looked up. "That's what keeps me going—the thought of riding Macallan again—and walking on the beach in Palm Beach."

"What do the doctors say?"

"They don't say shit. I don't think they know yet."

"They're just being cautious. They are the world's best. My doctor in Paris tells me that healing is as much an art as a science. A lot will depend on you, Robert."

"Oh, that cheers me up.... Look at me...I can't get up...I'm having terrible dreams—my son, a terrorist, blowing up the White House, killing everyone." *Where is My Hanh?*

"Hey, keep your mind on riding Macallan and walking on the beach. The man I know will do both again. I'm sure of it."

"Pierre, I don't know that man anymore," Robert said as he waved him away and kept staring off to avoid eye contact. He closed his eyes, his spirit sapped.

The following day, as the sun set on the Puy de Dome, the largest dormant volcano in the region, the light flickering on the fields outside Robert's window, My Hanh arrived at the clinic.

She walked up to the traction bed and gently placed her hand on his shoulder.

"You."

"Me."

"Thank you for coming."

"Oh, Robert, you're suffering..."

"Everything hurts."

She stood by the bed in silence.

"How long are you staying?"

"Two days...I was hoping to stay longer, but I have to get back to Hanoi."

"Only two days? I'll try to be on my best behavior."

"That would be nice...different, but nice!"

"Right!" They laughed. It was his first laugh since the shooting.

"When I woke up at the hospital in Paris, were you—?"

"Yes...you were not yourself."

"That's diplomatic...I think I insulted—

"Everyone—"

"What about An...is he?"

She paused and looked at him, perplexed. "Is he?"

"Is he...did I...? My memory...I—"

"No, no...you really don't remember, do you?"

"I tried." He looked away.

"You took a bullet for him, Robert. You saved him."

"Why didn't you tell me?"

"I told you at the hospital."

Robert closed his eyes, stunned. "I was so mixed up...the apartment...the swirling lights, the struggle...the blast...I thought I had killed him." He opened his eyes again and looked at her. "...and I thought I saw—"

She took her black scarf and wrapped it around her head as if it were a mask, leaving only her eyes visible. "Does this help you remember?"

Robert tried to move, but he was held in place by the straps that secured him to the table beneath the mattress. "It *was* you!"

"Yes. I led the commando group that rescued you and An."

A jumbled neuron in Robert's memory sparked... *The young girl she helped on the path next to Hoan Kiem Lake—the chop with her palm that broke three boards...*

He smiled and shook his head in amazement. "*You* saved us...why the sad look, then?"

"I had to resign my command. I disobeyed a direct order not to carry out the mission."

"You sacrificed your career for An and for me," he said as he looked at her and studied her face. He turned his head and looked out the window at the lush fields now illuminated by the moonlight. "Where is An?"

"After the rescue, he went into hiding. He saw you take the bullet for him. He didn't know about this part of my life either. I'd kept it from him for his safety. From everyone."

"What did he say to you?" Robert asked.

"He didn't speak. The shock on his face— He slipped out of the apartment and disappeared. I have not heard from him since. Bertrand thinks he's back with Ramzi. Every intelligence agency in the West is searching for them. It's said they're planning something big. Nobody knows what, or where."

He looked at her and opened his eyes wide as another memory returned. "I told him who he was...about you and me...and Bertrand."

She looked down with a sharp intake of breath, then pausing. "You did right. You were trying to save yourself and him. I was wrong to keep him from you and you from him all those years."

"So you finally admit it...a little late, but—"

"I spent some time with your father at the hospital. He was shaken by what you said to him—the sign with both your names—he said he didn't realize—"

"Nonsense. Of course, he did. He must have."

"Yes, but beneath his insensitivity, there is humanity. I sensed it. Someone in his past must have hurt him like he hurt you."

"What else did you talk about?"

I told him what a friend you had been to our country. I told him about your visit to Hanoi, about our talks to establish reconciliation between our countries. He knew nothing of this."

"I kept it secret like I was told."

"So you have your secrets, too!"

"Yes."

"I also spoke with Allen at the hospital. You should know, without his help, I could not have mounted the rescue. I had to push him, but when I did, he went outside the chain of command for you just as I did. He gave me intercepts and surveillance. He left them in the hole in the trunk of our tree in the Tuileries Garden."

Robert's eyes opened wide. The memories poured out. *The tree where we made love...* "Allen found us?"

"No, Pierre found you. Someone gave him the precise details of your location—accurate down to the exact number of steps from the curb to the front door of the apartment."

Robert smiled. *Someone...the nasty climb up and down the roof. It worked!*

"It was a garbled message left on his answering machine, the voice distorted, but the details led us to you."

"Did you speak to Andi?"

"Yes. You should know she was quick to defend you, telling me and the others that your outbursts were likely the result of post-operative psychosis. She covered for you, and that showed loyalty—especially when you acted so badly."

"And you? How are you?" Robert asked softly.

"Oh, I'm well. I do what Chairman Vo assigns me, and I accept my place. I'm trying not to be that ambitious girl anymore. I listen more to the voice in me that says the office I hold is less important than the good I can do. This is a change for me. It's the sword I still struggle to return..."

He looked at her. "You know, before that trip to Hanoi, seeing you again, meeting our son, I don't think there was a person on the planet I would have taken a bullet for."

She reached out and offered her hand. Without hesitation, he took it. And for the first time since his hospitalization, he felt the warmth of human touch from someone he cared for and who cared for him. It felt good.

Chapter 19

The next day, My Hanh returned to Robert's bedside. She brought him a container.

"Where did you get *pho ga* in Auvergne?"

"There's a village not far from here. It's called Noyant-d'Allier. After our nation's victory at Dien Bien Phu, hundreds of people had to flee Vietnam, and the people of this village opened their hearts to them. Half the town is Vietnamese. There's a pagoda, Vietnamese food, women and men wearing Áo dài.' It's like home."

They shared the *pho ga* and spoke of old times in Paris and their more recent time together in Hanoi. She filled him in on the progress that had been made toward the reconciliation since they had each filed their reports. Their work was bearing fruit, although they agreed it would still take a few more years.

In the afternoon, the doctor presented Robert with an option for a tough regimen of physical therapy instead of a more dangerous surgery. If the physical therapy did not take, they could do the operation later. It would be hard work and painful. My Hanh encouraged him to do it.

Robert remembered more of what had happened in the apartment on Place des Vosges. He recounted his conversations with An and how he thought they had connected, but he could not be sure. Something in him wanted to believe that one day he would still have a chance to reach his son. My Hanh listened, but she told him there was little reason to believe this could ever happen. He knew it too, but he hung on to the hope.

With her there, his spirits rose, and so did his curiosity about work, the acquisition, the things that used to drive him. They spoke about what would be next in his life and in hers. There was still a great deal he wanted to accomplish in his field—bringing quality programming to every major city in America. She wanted to use her waning influence to become an advisor to the commando group. She would find satisfaction in mentoring the young warriors as they trained for the unit.

My Hanh managed to turn two days into three. On her last day, the doctor entered Robert's room and told him that his team was working on a new laser technique to fuse severed spinal tissue. It held promise for him. The news buoyed him and brought cheers from her.

"Can you stretch three days into four?" he asked.

"I can't. I received a telegram from home. My mother is ill. I need to return in the morning."

That night, they had dinner in his room. After, they sat and looked at the sunset over the mountains.

"When I get out of here, I'm going home, too…to see my father," he said.

"To bury the sword, or to wield it?"

"I don't know…. I don't know what's possible."

"Well, sometimes knowing that you don't know is a good thing," she said.

"Any advice?"

"Three things." She reached for his hand and fell silent to gather her thoughts.

"Alright, what?"

"First, when you see him, take a breath and admit to yourself that you are suffering."

He looked at her quizzically. "Right…"

"Find the courage to tell him or show him."

He looked down, skeptical. "Right…"

"Then, find a way to tell him that he is suffering, too."

"You think he is?"

"I know he is—that's what's below his armor, and yours."

"So we're both victims…"

"Yes. And tell him you need his help. You want to understand him."

"I'll probably get punished..."

"You will, and you must bear it like you have the pain in your body."

"And after?"

"Become a refuge for him so he can become a refuge for you."

"You make that sound easy."

"It is, Robert—if you open your heart. You might also want to apologize for what you said at the hospital."

"Oh...right." He clasped her hand tightly as they watched the finale of the sunset before them. The temperature dropped. It was time to close the windows. The nurses entered the room to give Robert his medications and to announce that the time had come for all visitors to leave. My Hanh rose from her chair. She gently kissed him—their first kiss on the lips of the visit—and rather than engaging in a long goodbye, reached into her bag and handed him a letter. He took it and smiled at her as she turned to leave the room and head back to Vietnam.

"Good luck with your mother," he said.

"Same with your father." And she was gone.

Robert asked the nurse to put the unopened envelope on the dresser and lean it against the wall. For the next several days, he looked at it in the morning when he rose and, in the evening, before he went to bed. He wanted the message inside to age like a fine wine in its bottle. In a remote corner of his mind, he worried that it might contain something bad, another hurtful goodbye. When the moment came to read it, he would know. Until then, he would wait. And think of her.

The intensive therapy began, then continued unabated. The laser treatments progressed. He started to feel his legs and his feet again. He wiggled his toes. Pierre visited on weekends, and Robert asked him to take him to Noyant-d'Allier. He missed My Hanh. The clinic provided a special van equipped to carry Robert's wheelchair and emergency medical equipment. The driver was a trained nurse. Pierre pushed the wheelchair as they visited the pagoda in the town center and stopped for lunch at a Vietnamese restaurant. He saw that even talking of her gave him strength.

Late that afternoon, upon their return to the clinic, Robert discovered that the letter was missing from the dresser. He panicked and called for the nurse, who came quickly and assured him that the cleaning crew had simply placed it inside the drawer because they had polished the wood surface of the dresser. The nurse took the letter from the drawer and handed it to Robert. He tore it open.

My dear Robert,

Our visit was magic for me. The letter I wrote to you long ago when I left you in Paris was not honest, so I want to make sure this one is. I feel the connection in my heart to you now as I did then, but I don't know how to react at this point in our lives. I am returning home to think about this and to speak to my mother, who has always guided me in the important moments of my life. I will tend to her through her illness. I will meditate and commune with the forests of the Buc Son Valley, which, like Auvergne, is a place where nature can add its wisdom to everything. I will look into my heart. It will help me chart my course. My political dream is over. My marriage to Bertrand is a warm friendship that I must respect. I will speak to him about his needs, and I shall consider mine, too. I will make choices that include everyone who depends on me and on whom I depend. Where that will lead, I do not know, but I tell you today as I did long ago that you are in my heart. Our love burns inside me. And I know when we are apart once more, I shall long for you. I shall long for the light my father saw in you, the light I now see. Good luck with your father. Please remember my advice. Keep me with you,

My Hanh

Chapter 20

My Hanh's letter rocketed his spirits into the stratosphere. His commitment to regain his health soared. He longed to move his life forward. He wrote to Andi and asked her to come to France and report on the status of the acquisition. He wrote to Allen asking him to share any intelligence about An. He offered to privately fund another rescue mission if he could be located. He begged Allen to tell law enforcement to spare his son's life in the event he was caught. He would hire a team of lawyers to represent his son. He would do all that he could. He did not give up hope.

A few weeks later, Robert awoke to learn that Andi had arrived.

"Sorry I'm late," she said as she entered his room, carrying a large briefcase with reports on each of the fifty radio stations prepared by the company accountants and station staffs. When he heard her voice, he grabbed the wheels of his chair and swung himself around to greet her.

"How goes my hard-working partner?" he said and smiled.

"Just a little terrified," she said. "I'm not good with terrorist threats. They held our flight for three hours on the runway."

"Yes, they can be nerve-racking." *If she only knew!* "What's happened with the challenges?" he asked as he motioned her to put the reports on the table next to his hospital bed. She obliged and looked over at the bed.

"That's where you sleep?" she asked. "With trapeze bars dangling above your head?"

"It's been my home for many months, and I won't be unhappy when I can graduate to something more comfortable."

"When will that be?"

"Soon, I hope."

She pulled up a chair across from his wheelchair, and they got down to business.

"What's happening with Dellmore?" he asked.

"I don't know. Rumor is that the challenges may be withdrawn. Arent Fox is trying to confirm. Shall I proceed to closing, even if you're not yet back?"

Robert was shocked. He'd had no idea. "Yes, do that."

"You know, the rumors started soon after we found out you got shot."

Robert struggled to take this in. "Really?"

"Surprised me too. Maybe Dellmore decided life was too short."

"Yeah...maybe..."

"I always thought Paris was a safe city. Did they catch the bank robbers?"

"The bank robbers...oh, yes, they were arrested. I got caught in the crossfire. It was horrible."

"Yes, your friend Allen told me at the hospital. How is the rehab going?"

"I'm better. It's going well.... Um, about the hospital..."

"I've seen you worse," she said.

"So, we're okay?"

"Yes, okay."

"Good. Let's go over the reports," he said, snapping back to his former self. He questioned her in great detail about every aspect of the new stations, the formats, personnel, upcoming promotions, market position—everything, and she had a full command in providing the answers to each of his questions. At last, he asked her about how things were going with her boyfriend Jack Slate.

"We're good."

"How good?"

"Good enough that he wants me to divorce you so we can marry."

"Are you asking me for a divorce?"

"Did I say that?"

He was always good at reading her. *It's loud and clear.*

"I'm not going to get in your way with Jack. It won't end our partnership or our friendship if we divorce," he said reassuringly, which wasn't usually his way.

Uneasy going there, she changed the subject. "And what about you? Are you gonna be okay?"

"You know me, Andi. I'll land on my feet. No pun intended."

"Jesus, Robert..." She looked him in the eye. "I want you to find happiness. The kind we never seemed to manage." She patted him gently on the knee.

He smiled. *I can feel it.*

Chapter 21

The winter turned to spring, and outside the white fields turned green again—a renewal of the seasons in a region of world-re-nowned agriculture. Pierre continued to visit regularly, providing encouragement and bringing treats from the culinary bounty of Auvergne—dry cured sausages, *sausisse seche,* cheeses of the region, *Cantal, Saint Nectaire and Fourme d'Ambert,* and a local favorite, *aligot,* a heavenly combination of whipped potato and cheese. One spring day, Pierre returned with a box of *millefeuille* baked by the pastry chef at the Crillon and a special surprise.

The horse had been at the Longchamp Racecourse in Paris since October and had won the celebrated *Prix de l'Arc de Triomphe.* Pierre had worked an agreement with a local farmer to care for the animal and to bring him to the field each day just outside the French windows next to Robert's bed. Macallan would linger there, and on the warm days with the windows open, the magnificent thoroughbred would thrust his head inside and neigh, as if to reach out to the friend who had always confided in him.

The people in the surrounding farms and villages were amused at the sight of this world-class specimen, winner of the greatest races, connecting with its owner. Robert understood that in other places it might have seemed strange. But this was Auvergne, and the farmers of this remote region, producers of food for the nation and the world, were rooted in the land, the mountains, the lakes, and the animals that inhabited them. They had an uncommon comfort with the mysteries of nature, *un bon sens paysan,* which left them grounded, unflappable, nonchalant, and according to folk lore, they were made special by the ancestral vibrations of the volcanos that surrounded them. A horse wanting to connect with its owner was just another turn of nature. Robert came to love Auvergne, a land and a people that helped to heal him.

He rarely got mail, having cut himself off from the world. When he got a small package from Andi, he was surprised—not that the note inside asked him for a divorce—but that she sent him the ring he had bought for My Hahn twenty-three years before to give her in the Tuileries Garden. He had kept it in the top section of the jewelry box on his dresser all these years. She knew what it meant to him and wrote, "You'll need this now. You're free. Give it to your true love." He never loved Andi more than when he read those words.

This wasn't the only bright light in his recovery. The new laser procedure helped to speed the healing. His pain diminished further. More importantly, he came to believe that with hard work, he might walk again. He renewed his determination. The bad dreams that had haunted him happened less frequently and with less intensity. He never stopped thinking about My Hanh and about An. He wondered where his son was and felt deeply troubled that he might still be with Ramzi planning an act of terrorism. At the same time, he realized that there was nothing he could do about it, and he began to accept that his son might remain lost to him.

At last, the doctors scheduled the date of his discharge. On the eve of his return to a new life, he decided on two important steps. First, he sent the ring to My Hanh in the hope that it would keep him in her thoughts. It was his way to invite her to share the future in any way that worked for her. Next, he made preparations to keep his word to himself and to My Hanh to visit his father. He knew that whatever life he sought to live going forward, it would not be complete without reconciling with Irwin. He needed to let go of his anger—to be set free—before he could move ahead. It was time to return the sword.

Robert asked Pierre to take a leave of absence from the Crillon to accompany him home and help him settle back in his Palm Beach mansion. Andi had moved out. There was much to do. He threw himself into the work of making the house wheelchair friendly. He hired a New York architect to design the changes and installed elevators, including one to bring him from his bedroom down to the beach. He pulled down the temperature-controlled, custom-built display of his most precious bottle of *Macallan* in the foyer of the mansion—one that had set the record for the highest price ever paid—and replaced it with the photo of young An that My Hanh had given him in Hanoi. He placed it in a simple silver frame and hung it above a wooden table, a replica of the table with the gold inlays, hand-painted flowers, and intricately carved legs from Ngoc Son Temple on Jade Island where he and My Hanh had negotiated. On the table, he placed a bowl of fresh fruit, an urn for incense, and a vase of purple hyacinth, symbols of his sorrow and regret. *The only Jew on Palm Beach with a shrine!*

Among all that he had to do and adjust himself to, Robert called and arranged to meet his father. His specially equipped limo pulled up to the entrance of the Breakers Hotel, and Pierre loosened the clamps that held his wheelchair in place and wheeled him out the back of the vehicle. Irwin waited, pacing at the entrance to greet his son. Robert tapped his index finger on the arm of the chair. He worried about how his father would react to the scene at the hospital. Pierre pushed the wheelchair, and the three of them walked toward the ocean pathway. The sea was pristine blue, the breeze roiling the crowns and fronds of the palm trees whose trunks grew leaning into the wind, toward the ocean to provide protection.

"What the fuck were you doing over there? Hanging out with commies again? I should have known better. You're pathetic," Irwin began.

Pierre placed his hand on Robert's shoulder to steady him. He looked back at his friend, grateful for the signal that he was not alone. This was the punishment he had expected. He heard My Hanh's cooling words in the hot breeze. *"You must bear it like you have the pain in your body."*

"Irwin," Robert responded, looking up at his father. He had planned to call him Dad, but the broadside quashed that. *I'm suffering, alright!* He spoke slowly. "The money was to pay ransom for me and for my son. I was kidnapped—taken against my will."

"And you needed *my* money? I raised you right, put a roof over your head, sent you to the best schools, even to Paris to study, and what did you do with it? You fell in love with a communist, and worse, the daughter of our enemy. And you helped them! You took the side of the enemy. Not our side. You brought this on yourself."

"Irwin, look at me, I'm in this chair now—"

"You'll get no sympathy from me. None—and what about this son? You had a son, and you never told me about it. That's you. That's you."

Robert paused to measure his words. "I'll tell you about him...but first, do you remember what you told me when we flew to Montana on the fishing trip, and you asked me to join you in the business?"

"I don't remember. Or I put it out of my mind with all my other painful memories."

"*Your* painful memories?" Robert asked.

"I've got my share..."

"Like what happened with your older brother Marty? Why did you stop talking to him? Why did you skip his funeral?"

"He was pathetic, too! I worked my ass off to build our coin machine business so we could put a down payment on a radio station and move up in the world, become something, broadcasters—somebodies instead of nobodies—and what did he do? He fired me. Threw me out. No reason. He just looked at me and said, 'Things have changed.'"

"You never told me about this..."

"No, I never told anyone," Irwin said, an aggrieved look on his face.

"That must have hurt—"

"You can't fucking imagine."

"Become a refuge for him so he can become a refuge for you..."

"It must have been terrible."

"I spent three days crying. Your mother thought I had had a breakdown. I almost did."

"How did you pull yourself up?"

"I just figured I would show the bastard. I would get out there on my own and do better, which is exactly what I did."

Robert sat dumbfounded at the realization that what his father had done to him, his older brother Marty had done to Irwin. *My Hanh nailed it... "Someone in his past must have hurt him like he hurt you."*

"On our trip to Montana, you said that every Jewish father with a business secretly wants his son to join him, wants his son's name up on the marquee alongside his own. You told me that was your dream, that together we could grow the business so large it would take care of all our needs. And you told me that *one day*, when you retired, I would take charge. Do you remember?"

"Yes, yes..."

"And do you remember what you told me when you put Dick in charge?"

"No...what did I say?"

"You said, 'Things have—'" Robert held his breath and looked at his father, who lowered his head and swallowed hard. It was clear by the look on his face that these memories had struck a nerve. "So we have both felt the same pain," Robert whispered.

"Damn," Irwin said as a gust of wind blew up and a bellowing wave crashed almost to the edge of the concrete path.

"My son—his name is An. It means 'peace' in Vietnamese. He was born to my first love, My Hanh, from my year abroad in Paris. You met her at the hospital. I didn't know she had given birth to our child. She never told me. When I found out, something changed in me—the thought that, like you, I had a son. Only he's a son with a life so different than mine, than ours, you couldn't even imagine..."

"Whatever the differences, he's still your son," Irwin said.

"Does that go for you and me?"

"Yes, damn it...I guess it does," he said. "Where is he?"

"I don't know. I've lost him. I never really had a chance—tried to reach him, but I didn't have enough time." A tear fell down Robert's cheek and blew off in a gust of wind.

"Shit, there's no use looking back."

"For An and me, or for you and me?"

"For all of us."

"But if you did look back, you might see yourself as that little boy, the youngest of five brothers who fought to be noticed, to mean some-thing, to matter," Robert said.

"Marty was my older brother. I revered him. I depended on him. When he fired me—"

Robert saw Irwin's face tighten. He braced himself for another storm. But his father reached down and placed his hand on the arm of the wheelchair, signaling to Pierre to stop. He

turned to his son. "I fired *you*, didn't I?

Robert nodded.

"When you passed over me and named Dick your successor, I became just like you—a lean, mean accomplishment machine. I set out to prove that you made the wrong choice, that I was worthy, and I have suffered just like you."

"Find the courage to tell him or show him."

Irwin lifted his head and looked out at the ocean, and then slowly lowered his gaze back to his son. Robert saw that he was struggling to find words. Irwin cleared his throat. "My friends at the club—the guys with the real money—teased me about you. They called you a leftist, said you helped the communists. One heard that you were just in Hanoi, helping them again. They threw your history in my face. Their sons were in the military. Dick was a decorated Marine. They said patriots wouldn't want a lefty operating the largest group of radio stations in America."

"You couldn't see through that?"

Irwin looked down.

Robert asked Pierre to wheel him over to a bench at the edge of the beach and signaled that he needed a moment alone with his father. His friend stepped aside, leaving the two of them alone. Robert looked at his father and said, "Dad, take a look at this letter." He handed him the classified letter Allen had found. It was from the President of the United States, Lyndon Johnson. Irwin took the letter and held it firmly in his hand so it would not blow away. He reached into his pocket and pulled out his reading glasses, and sat down on the bench just beside Robert's wheelchair and the crashing waves of the Atlantic. When he was through, he slapped the letter down on his knee and stood up to face Robert.

"By God, you were a double agent!" Irwin exclaimed.

"I was. I worked for the President of the United States. I worked to end a war. I worked because ending the war was something rooted in my values. It was difficult. It cost me more than you can imagine, and ultimately, it failed. *I* failed. I couldn't stop the war. But as I look back, I can at least take satisfaction in the fact that I tried."

"Why didn't you tell me?"

"I took an oath not to tell anyone for twenty-five years. It's only been twenty-two. But I got clearance to tell you."

"And the rumors now about you and Hanoi?"

"They're true, and I can't talk about that either, but you should know that the man who sent me lives in a white house, and he's not a leftist." Robert looked up and saw tears welling in his father's eyes. "Let's get out of here. I think it's about to rain."

"Yes," his father said, wiping his eyes.

Robert signaled for Pierre to come over. He pushed the wheelchair back to the hotel entrance, and Irwin walked next to them. They didn't say another word, but when they reached the open rear door of the limo, Irwin, still holding the letter, handed it back to Robert.

"No, Dad, you keep it. I want you to have it."

Irwin took back the letter, and for the first time in decades, kissed his son goodbye.

Thank you, My Hanh!

Chapter 22

Robert sat nervously in the wheelchair outside the conference room at his corporate headquarters on the one hundred and sixth floor of the World Trade Center. This was his first board meeting in more than a year. He was filled with anticipation. He had been back for six months in Florida, taking emergency calls only, but this was his first time at headquarters. Pierre had flown in and stood behind him. He asked gently, "Are you ready?"

"Ready."

He began to push the chair forward into the room, but Robert raised his hand. "I'll take it from here."

He rolled himself into the room, greeted Andi, and looked at the others sitting nervously at the enormous table. These were the people who'd helped him build the company, the people of his past, each now wondering about the future. The rumors about what had happened to Robert had spread within the industry. All knew what they had read in the newspapers—the CIA cover story that he had been shot during a Paris bank robbery. All knew about the injury and how it impacted his outer life, but none knew the state of his inner life. Robert rolled himself to the head of the imposing, twenty-foot mahogany table. The members of the board fell silent. The last time they had gathered in this room was to ratify the largest radio station acquisition in American broadcast history—fifty stations in the top fifty markets added to the Samberg Broadcast Group. In Robert's absence, Andi had taken charge.

He arrived at his customary place at the end of the table and grasped the gavel in front of him. It was a scene he had played out a thousand times before, but this time he knew it would be different. Before he could gavel the start of the meeting, Andi stood and applauded. She was joined by her new husband, Jack Slate, who stood when she did, followed to their feet by the regional heads of the station groups, the company vice presidents, the corporate attorney from Arent Fox, the finance consultant from Cantor Fitzgerald, the accountant from Deloitte, and a special guest, who had never attended before—Irwin Samberg. Robert looked at his father, standing and clapping. *Never thought I'd see the day.*

As the applause crescendoed, he pounded the gavel with a force that left no doubt he was taking charge. The board secretary read the minutes of the last meeting. During the reading, Robert looked again at his father. The last time he had seen him was on the beach. He had sent him a handwritten invitation to the meeting but was not sure he would come. He smiled at him, and Irwin returned the greeting. He looked at his face—the lines on his brow, the grey hair, the gauntness of a man in ill health, and, at last, felt no anger. After the minutes were read, an awkward silence filled the room, then Robert spoke.

"A great deal has happened in this company over the past year." He paused. "You've

accomplished a lot—for our stations, our listeners, our advertisers. There is no other radio group out there like this one—and that's because of you."

He paused and looked at the faces around the table, each hanging on to his every word. It was a center of attention that in the past had always empowered him, yet at this moment, he felt oddly uncomfortable. The glare of the spotlight masked something soft and new within him, a comfort in quietly taking his place among others rather than feeling compelled to win their approval.

Robert continued but noticed that his voice trembled, an unsteadiness that no one in the room had heard before. "A great deal has happened with me, too—this chair for one thing." He looked down and searched for the right words, then looked up again. "Winston Churchill once said, 'There is nothing more exhilarating than to be shot at without result.'" He looked down again. "I wasn't so lucky."

They all looked on in stone silence. Robert sat up straighter. He sought to move on from an awkward moment to something more positive. "We've been together a long time. I pushed myself. I pushed all of you. Sometimes because that's what it took to get us here. Sometimes, because that's the only thing I knew how to do. And look at us now, up here, on top of the world."

Robert waved toward the wall of windows and the majestic sight of New York City below. "You got us here, and I know you'll keep us here." He paused again to gather his thoughts. "For me, there are some new challenges—different ones." His voice broke. He swallowed, collected himself, and continued. "Since I last saw you, I found a son I didn't know I had, and as hard as I tried, I couldn't reach him. He's gone." Glancing at Andi, he added, "I found a woman I once loved and thought I had lost." She reached over and touched his hand to convey her support. No one had ever heard him speak like this.

"Dad, I'm happy you're here today. With the acquisition, your company became part of mine." He locked eyes with Irwin and paused.

I have shown you what I needed you to see. And today, I lay down my sword. I want to show you something more important. I want to show you my heart. I forgive you, as I hope you'll forgive me.

"I could not have done this without the benefit of what you taught me." He paused again.

The apple didn't fall far from the tree. But make no mistake, it's a different apple.

"As far as I'm concerned, we've come home, we're together, just as you once wanted—the sign, Samberg and Son, now hangs in this room."

And at last, in my heart.

Robert paused and looked at Dick Dellmore. "Dick, the note you wrote to me in Paris after you met with Pierre.... he brought it to me in rehab on a day when I felt all was lost. There were many like that. It wasn't going well. I was tired and ready to give up. And I read your words—how you saw things differently, how you saw me differently. You just can't imagine how this lifted me at the moment I needed it most. It helped me reclaim a part of myself, and all the injuries, recent and long ago, just vanished. Robert paused again. He looked at his father.

I'm not giving up on us, Dad. Or my son. Or the woman I love. Or...myself.

He reached down and flipped away the foot braces beneath the chair and, in a mighty effort, thrust himself upon his feet, holding the table in front of him.

"I will walk again." He stood there silently and looked around the table at the faces frozen in shock.

How could I have spent so much time, accomplished so much, yet know so little of these people?

Everyone in the room sat on the edge of their chairs.

"I know this will come as a shock to all of you, but today, I'm resigning as board chair, retiring...and I'm appointing Andi to take my place at the head of the company—Hell, she's already doing it," he added. By now, clearly straining to stay on his feet, he looked at her and said pointedly, "I know she can handle it." Then proclaimed, as if apologizing for years of doubting her, "She always has. We wouldn't be here without her." Then Robert lifted his hands from the table and began to clap. Jack Slate quickly stood and clapped, too. Then Irwin, Dick Dellmore, and the others. The applause continued, and the nervousness in the room melted away.

Robert lowered himself back into the chair. He gazed out the windows to the cityscape below. Then turned and thanked each member of the board for their contributions to the success of the company. This was another surprise, something he had never done before. Finally, he turned to Andi. "There's no one more qualified. I know you'll do me proud." She beamed. Then, he motioned to Pierre, who stood in the corner of the room, to come to him.

"Well, I'm off. As of this moment, I'm retired, so please don't call me. *Call Andi.* She'll handle it. She handled me, didn't she? Watch yourself, Jack." As the room broke into laughter, he looked at her with more love than they had ever had—the love of true friends. "I wish you all the best. Now, I have a plane to catch."

"Where are you going?" Irwin asked.

"Back to Paris." Andi stood again and cheered, joined by the others.

"What's in Paris?" his father asked.

"I don't know yet…I'm hoping my heart."

Robert smiled—a smile anchored in his heart, glowing through his eyes. It was a smile no one in the room had ever seen on his face before. It was the light.

Chapter 23

With a sense of relief bordering on euphoria, Robert boarded the Concorde for Paris. He carried an unopened letter from My Hanh that had arrived that morning. He handed it to Pierre, telling him to hold it until they arrived at the hotel. He would read it in the room. It was her response. *What if she didn't want the ring? What if it was too much? Was my invitation too pushy?* On the flight, it was all he could think about. They headed by limo to the hotel on the Place de la Concorde. It was a cold day with a clear sky. As the limo pulled up and the uniformed doormen of the Crillon swarmed around the car, Robert noticed Ambassador Curley and CIA Station Chief Bill Brooks waiting outside at the hotel's entrance.

"You came all the way across the street to greet me?"

"Let's grab a coffee," Curley said. Brooks and Curley followed as Pierre wheeled him through the hotel to the restaurant where the maître d' welcomed them warmly and showed them to a private table. Unlike other hotel guests, Robert didn't need to check in. It was as if the owner of the chateau had returned home after a long absence. It had been more than a year.

"To what do I owe this honor?" he asked as Pierre rolled his wheelchair up to the table and the others sat down.

Curley looked squarely at Pierre. "We need a moment in private, please." Pierre looked at Robert who signaled for him to step away.

"It's good to be back," Robert said. "Tell me—"

"Hold on," Curley said, placing his right index figure up to his lips. Brooks pulled a small radio wave scanner from his briefcase and panned it around.

"We're clear." Brooks nodded at Curley. "Nobody's listening."

"Robert, we received a top-secret cable from State—from Allen Hoffers on behalf of Secretary Baker—that they want to consult with you on the opening of the MIA office in Hanoi and the work of a new Senate select committee on POWs and MIAs. There are also peace talks underway here in Paris on Cambodia. Vietnam still has troops there, and we need to get them out to clear the way for opening diplomatic relations. There are other issues, the trade embargo and the travel restrictions. They want to consult you on those, too."

"Is that all?" Robert said with a wry look. "You guys know I just retired, right?"

"Robert, Allen also wanted you to know…"

"Know what?" Robert asked, an edge of anticipation in his voice.

Curley lowered his voice. "About An."

Robert frowned. "Oh, no…please don't tell me…"

"No, no, he's all right…" Brooks added.

"If you call working with Ramzi to plan a terrorist strike all right," he said. "That's what I heard, but wouldn't you guys know?"

Leaning close to Robert's ear, Curley whispered slowly, enunciating each word, "It's true, but there's something more…"

"What?"

"He's with us…"

As his jaw dropped, Robert felt a thunderclap of emotions. He took a breath, allowed the news to sink in, and when it did, the sensation of pure joy surged in his heart.

"My god! He went undercover. But how did he—"

"There was only one person left alive to tell Ramzi what had happened in the apartment," Brooks explained. "We found An outside, after the rescue. He was wounded, shaken, running away, unsure of what to do. We took him to the embassy and treated his injury. We set up a place for him to stay in the security wing. At first, he wouldn't speak. Allen flew in and brought with him the one person in America who we knew might be able to reach him—Sidney Rittenberg, a Chinese linguist in the Army who had stayed in China after the revolution and who had become a friend of Mao Zedong. He shared stories with An about Mao's interest in America—the only foreign country that had really fascinated and interested him and one he had greatly admired. He told him how Mao had invited left-wing Americans to his home to sit and chat—a special privilege he had offered to no other nationality, only the Americans. He told him that Mao had once confided in him that in the beginning, he had thought Jeffersonian democracy was the future for China, and he explained how and why he had had to give up on Western-style democracy and had turned to Lenin. He told An that in his view, had America reached out and developed ties with Mao and with China in these early days, there might not have been wars in Korea and in Vietnam."

"And this turned him?" Robert asked.

"No," Curley said. "What turned him was when Allen handed him the CIA file on My Hanh—the heroics of her female commando group in the war against the Khmer Rouge in Cambodia and against the Chinese in the border war. He saw her with the respect and admiration he had had for his fictional mother—only this was a mother who was real and who he came to realize loved him.

"But I think what finally closed the deal was when Allen handed him *your* CIA file from 1968. For the first time, he saw who his biological father was, how you put yourself at risk for peace in Vietnam, how you stepped up and helped to get the talks started to end the war. We didn't have much time. We needed to get him back to Ramzi with a cover story to avoid suspicion, and with a few more days of intense conversation, he came around. He's a double agent, like you were. He told us all he knew about the New York attack. Now he's with Ramzi, trying to find out exactly when and where the attack will take place."

"And afterward?" Robert asked. "Will you take care of him? He'll be a target."

"We'll put him in witness protection with a large stipend. Very large."

"After, how will I know how to track him?"

"He'll be given a code name. Mr. ...something very common, very

American. We'll let you know."

"Okay. Tell Allen and Baker that if my son is helping on the inside, I'll help on the outside. Does My Hanh know?"

"No one else knows, no one but Hoffers, Baker, the president, and the three of us."

"Can I tell her? It would mean the world to her."

"I'll run it up the chain, but I think you can guess the answer will be 'no.'"

Robert raised his right hand and placed it over his heart. Then he signaled to Pierre, who had been on the other side of the room preparing to resume his duties. As Pierre approached, Robert gave him a wanting look. Pierre knew what he meant. Robert was never more ready to read My Hahn's letter. He hated the thought of not being able to share the news of An, but he would keep it secret if he had to, still secure in his love—or maybe he wouldn't. *Damn secrets!* It was no longer about what she would or wouldn't say in the letter. He wanted her to be happy even if they lived a world apart. Pierre answered by lifting his head, looking up at the rooms above with a smile. "Go."

Robert handed him his coffee cup. "Cream on top."

"I'll send it up," Pierre replied, handing him the letter.

Filled with anticipation, he warmly thanked Curley and Brooks and rolled his wheelchair to the elevator, his mind flooded with thoughts. He wondered how he'd feel if she didn't mention the ring. *Maybe I should have sent her a new one. Cartier is right around the corner!* He wheeled along the ornate hallway up to the door of the presidential suite and rang for the valet to respond. *They're probably still unpacking.* Impatient, he braced himself, clasped the door handle tightly, and pulled himself up on his feet, just as the door to the majestic suite swung open. To his breathless surprise, the letter no longer mattered. Before him stood My Hanh, herself, a smile on her face, the ring on her finger, her arms and her heart wide open.

Robert's life had come full circle. He steadied himself, looked at her, and said, "We've got work to do." And with that, he took a big step forward.

Postscript

On February 26, 1993, a bomb exploded in a parking garage of the World Trade Center (WTC) in New York City—set off by a group of Middle Eastern terrorists. The FBI and New York City Police arrested most of the terrorists before they could leave the United States. Among those who escaped was the driver of the van containing the explosives, the mastermind of the plot—Ramzi Yousef. He had become one of the world's most wanted terrorists.

On February 3, 1994, President Bill Clinton *lifted* the nineteen-year-old US trade embargo of the Republic of Vietnam. The ban had been in place since North Vietnamese forces captured the city of Saigon in South Vietnam at the end of the Vietnam War. Clinton explained that he'd lifted the embargo primarily to encourage cooperative efforts between the US and Vietnam to discover the fate of American prisoners of war (POWs) and missing in action (MIAs) who had remained unaccounted for after the war. He cited the work by Senators John McCain and John Kerry as contributing to the effort. He also said that improved business relations between the US and Vietnam would benefit the economies of both nations.

One year later to the day, an informant presented himself at the residence of a US diplomat in Karachi, Pakistan, and claimed to have information about Ramzi Yousef's location. American security agents in Pakistan confirmed that the man was a former contact of Yousef, and they alerted Pakistani officials.

Four days later, Pakistani law enforcement officers and US security agents raided Yousef's room, waking him from a nap, and arrested him. The next day, he was flown to New York City for arraignment.

The informant received a $2 million reward, and Yousef was indicted for the 1993 World Trade Center bombing. He is serving a life sentence in solitary confinement with no parole plus 240 years at a federal "supermax" penitentiary located deep in the Colorado Rockies.

The mysterious informant who collected the reward was later identified as "Mr. Parker." Little was known about him. To this day, the Justice Department has refused to confirm or deny his identity or location. Apparently, he disappeared—allegedly in the witness protection program, living somewhere in the United States.

On July 11, 1995, the United States and Vietnam restored full diplomatic relations. Five years later, in 2000, Clinton became the first American head of state to visit Vietnam since the end of the war. He was warmly received. Standing just three miles from Jade Island on Hoan Kiem Lake—the lake of the Returned Sword—Clinton said, "The history we leave behind is painful and hard. We must not forget it, but we must not be controlled by it. Somehow, when our Vietnamese friends finally said they would accept us, and we said we would accept them, we were set free."

Amen.

Acknowledgments

Mission in Paris 1990 is the sequel to my first novel, *Hearts on Fire, Paris 1968*, published by Harmattan, Paris, in 2018 and soon to be published by the Ho Chi Minh City General Publishing House, Socialist Republic of Vietnam.

I could not have written this second book without the assistance of a number of talented and dedicated people. First and foremost, I thank the editors who contributed mightily to the effort, Christopher Noel, Ellen Brock, and my dear sister, Deborah Pearl.

I thank my test readers (and friends) Vo Thi Huong Lan in Vietnam and Cyril Dagouret in France. I offer special thanks to Lan for helping me to shape the character of My Hanh. If I got it right, she deserves much credit. If I got it wrong, the blame is entirely mine.

I thank two extraordinary writers, Jay Neugeboren and Joseph O Donnell, for their counsel and encouragement. Each has helped me to improve this work.

Special thanks to the Honorable Patricia Rochès, Mayor of Coren-les-Eaux, France, for sharing her knowledge of and love for her homeland, Auvergne, France.

Thank you to Xavier Preyen at Harmattan and to Nicolas Faroux for encouraging me and launching me on this adventure.

Thank you to my wife, Dr. Joann Hendelman, who has offered sound advice from the earliest outline, scratched out together in the north Atlantic onboard the Queen Mary 2, to the finished manuscript.

Special thanks to my talented daughter Jennifer Pearl, who designed the websites and social media platforms for *Hearts on Fire* and is on tap to do it again for this sequel. The fun we had recording the YouTube video campaign for the first book is a highlight of my life. I can't wait to do it again.

Thank you to Vietnamese journalist and author, Madame Hieu Constant, for her advice and counsel. Special mention as well to the Vietnamese Women's Museum in Hanoi, Vietnam, where I learned about the heroic women of Vietnam. The museum is a treasure.

I have dedicated this book to my mother, Helen Pearl, who inspires me every day with her love, wisdom and sense of humor. I thank the team of caregivers who keep her healthy and happy, Pam Dannelevitz RN, Millicent McFarlane, Esmine Findlayson, Veronica Edwards, Grace Watson RN, Liz Balon, and her doctor, Gabriella Goldstein, M.D.

I am ever mindful that I would not have been able to write this book without the hard work, dedication, and business acumen of Bill Reichel and his team at Reichel Realty and Investments in Palm Beach Gardens, Florida, who manage my real estate portfolio. They are the best!

And finally, among all who have helped me, I must offer the most heartfelt gratitude to my sister, Deborah, who has blessed this work with talent, insight, and a pen much more experienced and craftier than my own. Thank you, Debbie.

Palm Beach Gardens, Florida
December 16, 2020